"Thank you for an interesting evening."

Anna forced herself to speak as Mark pulled the car up outside the door at Orakau.

"Is that what you call it?" Mark snapped. "A useful diversion to fill the time. With Maurice holding your hand, murmuring sweet nothings in your ear."

Weakly Anna shook her head in protest. "I didn't encourage him. It didn't mean..."

"Didn't encourage him! You all but flashed neon signs at him." Mark moved, imprisoning her against the seat, his hand holding her head. His mouth descended, forceful and demanding. The kiss pulsed with their anger.

When he released her, Anna was shaking, outraged as much by his action as with her own response. From now on it would be war between them....

Books by Rosalie Henaghan

HARLEQUIN ROMANCE

These books may be available at your local bookseller.

Don't miss any of our special offers. Write to us at the following address for information on our newest releases.

Harlequin Reader Service
P.O. Box 52040, Phoenix, AZ 85072-2040
Canadian address: P.O. Box 2800, Postal Station A,
5170 Yonge St., Willowdale, Ont. M2N 6J3

Safe
Harbour

Rosalie Henaghan

Harlequin Books

TORONTO • NEW YORK • LONDON
AMSTERDAM • PARIS • SYDNEY • HAMBURG
STOCKHOLM • ATHENS • TOKYO • MILAN

Original hardcover edition published in 1985
by Mills & Boon Limited

ISBN 0-373-02751-6

Harlequin Romance first edition March 1986

CHAPTER ONE

IT was a beautiful day. The blue sky had painted itself on Wellington's inner harbour, the small wavelets too lazy to do more than slap themselves against the piles of the docks. Containers were being unloaded from a ship and the tall girl standing at the window of a high rise office block watched the progress with a knowledgeable eye. A ship's siren reminded her of her own work and she turned away from the fascination of the scene to the quiet elegance of her office. Her boss, Catherine Lester, had scheduled an agents' meeting for eleven-fifteen, and there was still the morning's mail to be completed. A buzz warned her that Mrs Lester had pressed her communication switch.

'Anna, dear, I'm running late with my notes. Would you make sure I have no telephone calls during the next ten minutes? Tell them I'm in Timbuctoo, if necessary.'

The tall woman smiled. 'Certainly, Catherine. Can I help in any other way?'

'Yes, bring me in the last meeting's full record, I want to check one of the agent's comments.'

Anna reached for the files and walked towards Catherine Lester's door. A moment later she returned, glanced at her telephones and decided to check her appearance. A small dressing room was beside her office and the full length mirror was mute testimony to the importance Catherine Lester placed on personal appearance.

5

Anna straightened her skirt and looked at herself critically. With her height and slim build, her hairstyle was a little harsh in its close, head-hugging style but Anna felt it made her look businesslike. Rapidly she combed the short brown hair into its neat lines and frowned when a curl curved round her ear. She combed it back, not approving of its frivolous appearance. It was always the same, cheeky curl and seemed to revel in its springing dance which no hairdresser could tame.

Satisfied it was flattened, Anna's eyes checked the subtle touch of bronze shadow highlight-ing her bright, intelligent brown eyes. She reapplied her lipstick, a soft pink which toned with her pink blouse almost hidden under the grey suit.

The 'phone on her desk buzzed and she moved swiftly to answer it, unaware of her natural grace. She would have been considerably taken aback to know that her effort to appear cool, sophisticated and impersonally efficient were totally ruined by the coquettish curl which sprang to its rightful place the minute she moved.

Picking up the receiver she flicked a switch and spoke in her well modulated voice.

'Good morning, Mrs Lester's office, Anna Heathley speaking.'

'Put me through to Catherine, please.'

Anna frowned. The business-like male voice was unfamiliar to her, yet he clearly knew Mrs Lester well to call her by her Christian name. She hesitated, then remembered her boss's instruc-tions.

'I'm sorry, I can't accept calls for Mrs Lester

at the moment. May I take a message or ask her to call you?'

'No, you can not. If Catherine's there, put me through.'

Anna glared at the unseen man. He spoke as if he had every right to order her around. The arrogant upstart! She had a good mind to tell him to get lost. She remembered her career book's golden rule, 'Treat everybody as if they are the big boss'. Forcing a smile into her voice she tried again.

'Could I ask who is calling, please?'

There was an angry snarl on the end of the line and she heard something muttered before he enunciated clearly.

'Mark Findlay.'

She frowned again and glanced at her clock. The man was asking for the moon, asking for Mark Findlay. She spoke calmly, more sure of her ground.

'This is the Wellington office of Mark Findlay International. Mrs Lester is the acting Chairman while Mr Findlay is in Tokyo. I am Mrs Lester's personal secretary. Can I help?'

'I said, put me through to Catherine. I didn't ask for a *Who's Who*!'

Anna's eyes flashed at the rudeness in the tone. Surely the wretched man could see she had her job to do.

'I'm sorry, Mrs Lester is unavailable. An important meeting . . .'

'Enough! You have wasted almost two and a half minutes of an international telephone call. It took you twenty seconds to answer from the main switchboard and now this delay is intolerable.

You wouldn't last ten seconds as my secretary, I'll tell you that! Now put me through to my sister, Mrs Lester.'

Anna stared at the 'phone as if it had suddenly grown two heads. Coming to, she spoke quickly, having realised the speaker's identity.

'Certainly, Mr Findlay.'

Her fingers pressed the buttons and she heard Catherine's 'phone buzz. It was answered immediately and she replaced her receiver, her hand shaking. There had been other 'phone calls from the managing director, but always there had been the distinctive tones of his secretary, Miss Penelope, before she had connected the call.

Since she had joined the company as Mrs Lester's personal secretary, Anna had heard a lot about the fabled, big boss. In the six months she had been with the firm she had been impressed by his business acumen and his razor-like ability. Some of the stories she had heard from his sister, Catherine Lester, who was running the company while Mark was setting up a new agency in Tokyo.

Catherine had told her that part of the company's success had been Mark's insistence on knowing the problems and the people he encountered. When setting up a new field he went himself, leaving the routine in his sister's extremely efficient hands.

'Man, I don't ever want to run into you in person,' she muttered as she glared at the 'phone. 'How can such a nice woman as Catherine Lester have you as a big brother? As far as I'm concerned you can stay in Tokyo.'

The knock on the outer door made Anna pull

herself together. The light on the 'phone glowed which meant that Mr Findlay and his sister were still talking. Anna decided she would have to group the agents and keep them in her office until the call was finished. It was just as well she had briefed herself.

Ten minutes later Anna ushered the agents to their seats and a smiling Mrs Lester began the meeting.

'I am very pleased to announce that my brother Mark is returning from Japan next week. He has successfully completed the office establishment in Tokyo and is satisfied it can now take its part in our chain. This makes the speed of imports much greater and we can expect a sharp increase on our figures from the area.

'Mr Findlay will be running the company from his home base just out of Christchurch as usual and informed me he will make a tour of the branches, to discuss future growth with all agents, soon after his return.'

Anna looked round the room at the expressions of pleasure and trepidation. Clearly Mr Mark Findlay made his impact felt wherever he went. Anna suddenly realised her boss was making another statement and her fingers flew, concentrating on the speech.

Exactly three quarters of an hour later the meeting finished and Anna looked at her notes. Mrs Lester looked at her with an enquiring smile.

'Come out for lunch? My treat. I'm so thrilled Mark is coming home again I feel I could turn cartwheels. Until he said he was coming I didn't realise how much I've missed him. This nine months has been hair raising. And you, my dear, young Anna, have been marvellous. I would have found it a great deal harder without your assistance.'

Anna smiled at her boss. 'I've enjoyed it. There's always so much of interest.'

'It is fascinating, isn't it?'

Mrs Lester snapped on a concoction of straw and flowers which matched the carefully shaded, blue-grey wing of her otherwise black hair. A sapphire brooch winked on the lapel of her tailored suit and matched the studs which glistened in her ears.

'You haven't met Mark, have you? I'm sure you'll impress him. He is remarkably observant and he remembers every detail with computer-like accuracy. A gift, I suppose, but a very useful one.'

She turned to pick up her handbag and Anna grimaced. She knew that she had no hope of impressing Mark Findlay after the disastrous start.

'Does Mr Findlay come here often?'

She asked it for reassurance; she would hate to work in an atmosphere where even the length of time it took her to answer a call was clocked.

'Mark? No, he tends to leave me alone. He knows I can cope, the darling, and just lets me get on with the local area. It means I can refer anything to him. The international scene demands his attention usually, so he finds it easier to work from home. I think in a way it's the right attitude. He is able to keep a distance on everything, so he can keep a perspective. Now, shall we go?'

Privately Anna thought that it sounded as if

Mark Findlay sat spiderlike in the centre of his empire with telephone and computers forming a web from which he could pounce on and gobble up any poor, unsuspecting insect. She remembered at school she had been labelled 'grasshopper' because of her long legs and she shivered; she had the strongest feeling that she would be his first victim.

'My husband's going to be thrilled Mark is returning. The darling man has been so good. My father warned him when he married me that he was marrying a business-woman. You would have liked my father, Anna. He was a very affectionate soul. Hopeless at the business, of course. Mark and I are more like our grandfather. He was the founder, the original Mark Findlay and I remember him as quite the sharpest tack around. He was so proud of Mark.'

'Has Mr Findlay a family?'

'No, he always declared he hadn't time to get married. I've tried; I've introduced him to some lovely girls but he seems to reduce them to noncompetents in one blistering second and that's scarcely the best way to start a relationship. He can be charming; I get so annoyed with him. I've tried telling him that it would help him in his business to have the right helpmeet, but even that doesn't make a scrap of difference. Sometimes I wonder if he does it deliberately to annoy me! It wouldn't surprise me in the slightest if he walked in here one day and said "This is my wife".'

'Well, I suppose your son will carry on in the business.'

'Unlikely. I would love to see it, but I have to

admit that he doesn't see a thing past his microscope.'

The sapphires flashed again as Mrs Lester sighed.

'He always tells me that as I enjoy my work I should be able to appreciate his interest in his work. He's right, of course. It would be wrong to force young people into a field they didn't want. My father would have been brilliant as a landscape designer but his father forced him into the business and made them both unhappy.'

'But how can you tell if a person has a gift?' mused Anna.

'Look at Mark. He was good at school but he never bothered. He saw no reason to work so he just coasted along.

'Then my grandfather made him help after school each night and copy out the main business points. Suddenly he was motivated. He realised that he needed to know a lot so he started making up for lost time. He began arguing with Grandfather and Dad. He went to University and did accountancy and law, specialising in our field and took over officially when my father retired. But to all intents and purposes he was running the company years before. Within five years he'd extended our agencies to double strength locally and established our first international office in Sydney. After that it was jet stream all the way.'

'Fascinating.'

'Now, my dear, you really must do justice to this superb food.'

Anna ate thoughtfully. She studied the woman opposite her but found it difficult to estimate her boss's age, she guessed she could be anywhere between forty-five or fifty-five. If her brother was even five years older that would make him fifty to sixty. If he was a crabby, old bachelor that would contribute to his bad temper on the telephone. She needn't worry, she'd hardly see him if he lived at Christchurch. They would have the width of Cook Strait and half the length of the South Island keeping them apart.

Three days later Anna picked up the chattering telex from the Tokyo office and read it through. She took it into Mrs Lester and silently handed it over.

'Oh! Brother!' Catherine said softly. 'Right, he wants a top flight secretary for six weeks; let's find one. I know there's no-one available at the office down there. Ring up an agency in Christchurch and see if you have any luck. It should be someone prepared to live on the job, work odd hours and with knowledge of our field. Make sure she is competent; he can't stand inefficiency, and discreet, she will be privy to some massive information.' She smiled. 'I imagine it will be a short list, don't you?'

Anna rang a Christchurch agency and passed the problem on. Within half an hour they rang back to say they had the perfect person. Anna checked the details and went into her boss with her report.

'Good,' Catherine Lester spoke. 'She sounds too good to be true! I feel that big brother of mine will think I've done well.'

Catherine picked up a file Anna had worked on earlier.

'These figures are better than last year. You've done a splendid job of presentation. It's much easier to read this way.'

They settled to work again and only as they stopped for afternoon tea did Mrs Lester pick up a small envelope on her desk.

'I brought these in to show you; old family photos. Then if even my brother Mark starts cutting you down, smile sweetly and think of these.'

She laid down two big pictures. The first was of a little boy with an inquiring gaze, his mop of dark curls running down his forehead. The second was of the same youngster, hand across his mouth, eyes scrunched up and he was clearly howling with rage; possibly because someone had snapped him in his birthday suit.

'He looks gorgeous! A real teddy bear.'

She remembered her telephone encounter. Mrs Lester was right. It didn't hurt any longer.

'How do you know?' she said with a smile.

'I know my brother. Normally his secretary Miss Penelope puts through his calls but she didn't the other day. Plus the fact that you've been jumpy each time I mentioned his name since that call and that's not like you.'

'He's not the only observant one in your family! I thought he was someone wanting to speak to Mark Findlay, not the man himself and I tried telling him he was in Japan.'

'What a joke! I hadn't realised you wouldn't know my brother's voice. I wish I'd heard you.'

Suddenly Anna could see the funny side of the situation too and she joined Catherine Lester in laughter.

'Now this next photo is of the house and you can see part of the gardens at Orakau. It's beautiful. Mark has his office in this section.

There's a lovely couple who have been with the family for years, absolute treasures, both of them. They have their own wing along here. On the other side is a small flat for Mark's secretary. She used to help my father and she is a wonder. That's why I was so surprised when I got Mark's telex. It's most unlike Miss Penelope to take a holiday away from her beloved home.'

Anna was still gasping at the mansion pictured. The sweeping lawns, the colouring of the trees, the parklike surroundings set off the residence of Mark Findlay and Company International.

'When Grandfather was older, Dad suggested we took the office to him and it was the smartest move we ever made. Mark keeps up the tradition. It suits him well, it's ideal for entertaining and he has the local branch as back-up if required. Oh dear! I've just thought of something. Miss Penelope's flat. It will be needed for the temp.' Catherine Lester's face fell.

'It seems like sacrilege to have someone prowling around her home, with all its knick-knacks.'

'Could the couple who look after the place pack them away?' Anna suggested.

'I suppose so,' Catherine Lester's face brightened. 'I know, we'll leave Miss Penelope's flat shut up and give the temp. my bedroom and lounge. For six weeks she could have meals with the others. Which reminds me. Book a flight down on Monday for me, will you, to return on Wednesday? I'll meet Mark when he arrives. He'll probably sleep for the first day in any case. That will give me time to meet this person the

agency has found. I'm afraid you'll have to alter
my schedule of appointments.'

It was a busy scene at the airport. Anna, having
seen off her boss, threaded her way through the
crowd. In the background loudspeakers announced the arrival of the direct flight from
Auckland. The scream of jets managed to
penetrate the area as the Christchurch-bound
plane prepared to move. Anna was grateful she.
didn't have to fly. She admitted that on the one
occasion before, she had been terrified.

Fishing in her handbag she took out a small
notepad and pen and some change for the
telephones. The bank of them were all occupied
and she found herself wondering about the
variety of people around her. When the first
'phone was clear some moments later, she dialled
the office. There were frequently parcels to be
collected at the airport and by checking now she
could save a run by the courier later. As
expected, a parcel had been sent from the
Palmerston North office. She made a note of its
freight number then stood dithering for a
moment thinking of her best route.

'If you're not satisfied with what the boyfriend
had to say think about it over there! Others wish
to use these telephones!' The male voice was
sharp and authoritative.

'I'm sorry,' Anna said hastily moving away.
Then she stopped, annoyed at the blatant attack.
Her telephone call had taken less than a minute
and she hadn't been standing beside it for long.
She turned to look at the man.

Tall and black-haired, he was already dialling.

He looked totally competent, Anna conceded, and she guessed he was accustomed to the world of jet set travel. His light jacket was of hand tailored silk and emphasised his rugged manliness. He was, she decided slowly, extremely good looking. His dark, curly hair fell over his forehead in a manner oddly at variance with the strong jawline and intelligent blue eyes. Eyes which were looking at her in a decidedly, hostile way. Anna suddenly woke up to the fact that she was staring and hurriedly walked off. She had enough to do without worrying about some rude stranger, she reminded herself sharply.

She went to the shop and purchased a couple of items, then went to the Island cargo bay. The parcel she had been asked to collect was not there, so she tried the main freight section.

She gave the attendant the number and he went off. A moment later he was back. 'Sorry. Not our section, could it be in the parcel pick-up area?'

'Please have another look, it should be here.'

Helpfully the man went off again. Anna became aware of a movement behind her and realised that because of her enquiry someone was being kept waiting. She turned to apologise and then rapidly turned back. She'd only needed one glance at the icy, blue eyes looking at her in disgust. It seemed an age before the counter attendant returned.

'Sorry, you're not having much luck are you? Now what can you tell me, we pride ourselves on our efficiency, especially for pretty girls.' He grinned at her but Anna was silently aware of the simmering rage of the man behind. The attendant spoke.

'You're sure it was sent yesterday? Let's see the number again.' He read it aloud.

'It's a direct flight so it couldn't have been unloaded at the incorrect station,' he commented.

'Doesn't that code denote the city depot?' The traveller spoke quietly but there was a note in his voice which implied they were both incompetents.

'Of course, must have been dreaming,' the counter attendant smiled easily but Anna felt crushed. After six months dealing in the field every day, she should have noticed the coding herself, and no doubt would have done if he had not interrupted her.

'Thank-you,' she said with shattered dignity and walked out of the area. Behind her she was aware of both men's glances; one of appreciation, the other scornful.

It took her a few moments to gather her thoughts enough to start the car's engine and drive it towards the main road. The big, luxury car was a pleasure to drive and she had to return it to the Lesters' home, once she had picked up the package and taken it to the office. Her trip there was uneventful and as she motored out to Lower Hutt she reflected that she was silly to let a small thing such as the bad temper of some unknown man upset her. In front of her would be a pleasant two days, with Catherine away she would have little to do and her boss had suggested she take the odd hour or two off. Her glance went to the rolled up towel which hid her latest bikini; the Lesters had a beautiful swimming pool with a perfect spot for sun bathing and Anna had several times taken advantage of the open invitation she had to use it.

Her pink lips formed a smile. It was a lovely, sunny day and for once she would be able to lounge in privacy. There were definite advantages for working for so nice a boss.

She eased off the accelerator and brought the car to a stop beside the large garage. The door was locked but it took only a moment to unlock it and drive the car inside. Removing her gear she shut it carefully and locked it then looked towards the house. She knew Mr Lester would be away at work and their son at the local university. Upstairs a window was open and a delicate white curtain fluttered like a flag of surrender. Anna smiled. She was going to surrender to the joy of having the place to herself.

'Wheeeeeee!'

She flung back her arms and ran to the pool changing area, discarding jacket and shoes, tossing each in the air and catching them expertly, laughter bubbling through her. She entered the small area and careful of her clothes placed them on the hangers provided, folded her underwear neatly, smoothing the lush embroidery of her petticoat on top. Humming an old song she picked up her towel wishing the mirror would reassure her as to the lines of her bikini. It was very daring, mere scraps tied with ribbons and she had bought it intending to wear it purely for private sunbathing. The Lesters' pool would be one of the few places she would dare to get it wet!

She dropped the towel by the edge of the pool and walked to the ladder. Tentatively she put one toe in and then withdrew it before immersing it again, a smile on her face. She hated getting wet all in one dive and it was lovely to take her time in total privacy. She did a little skip, then put her whole foot in and withdrew it and then sat down on the edge of the concrete and slowly put both legs in. Accustoming herself to the temperature she scooped a handful of water and dampened her face and felt its coolness glissade down her skin. She wriggled a little then slowly slipped into the pool.

The blue water sparkled around her and matched the diamonds in her eyes. She streaked to the far end of the pool, her arms cutting through the water, then she did a racing turn and slackened speed, swimming smoothly down the pool. Repeating the manoeuvre several times she gradually slowed and lazed in the water letting it roll over and around her, totally relaxed.

Only then did she climb out and flex herself, shaking her hair like a small, wet puppy, before lying on the towel to bake in the noon sun. The office knew where to find her and she could include her lunch hour, she told herself sleepily. She yawned catlike and wished she had brought a hat. Earlier she had put her sun tan lotion by her towel and now without opening her eyes she reached for it. Her hand flapped in a circle then touched something slightly hairy and warm.

She let out a yell of fright even as her eyes opened and she identified two sturdy legs. Hastily she sat up, her eyes wide as they lifted to the tall, tanned man with curling black hair and blue eyes.

'Looking for this? You seem to have a habit of misplacing things.'

The man stood smiling down at her, in his hands the bottle of lotion. Looking at his lithe, athletic body, naked apart from a pair of swimming trunks, Anna felt her heart pound as she recognised the man at the airport.

'Don't worry, everything else about you is placed in just the right order.' He looked at her slowly and deliberately. 'I'm pleased to have run into you again, I'm sorry I was such a boor at the airport. After flying for such a long time my manners tend to deteriorate.'

Again the lightning smile flashed. 'I'm ready to resume life again and quite happy to rub your back. That was what you had intended, wasn't it?'

He sat down beside her, ignoring her startled gasp and pushed her gently back against the towel. Anna was so surprised, she submitted as he stroked the lotion on, easing his fingers across her shoulders. She risked a glance at him again and decided that he must be one of the Lesters' friends.

He met her eyes and looked at her face critically.

'You'll get sunburn on your nose.' He put a large dollop of cream on it and Anna promptly squeaked as he pushed her down on the towel again.

'Patience, oh long-legged one, I have scarcely started.'

There was something very sensuous about the way he was rubbing her back, and she gasped when she felt him unfasten the strap of her bikini.

'Relax, you don't want to get oil on it or leave white marks across the skin.'

His voice was very deep and rang alarm bells all along her spine. A moment later he was lying beside her, kissing her shoulder and the nape of her neck, his hands caressing her expertly. Instinctively protecting herself with her hands holding her bikini top in place, she looked at him, her eyes wide with indignation.

'Who do you think you are? Please leave me alone.'

'Not likely! I told Catherine that the very next girl she dropped ever so thoughtfully in my path, I'd seduce on the spot! Maybe then she'll leave me to find my own female friends! You can give her the message!'

He chuckled and reached for her as easily as if he was reaching for a glass of wine he wished to enjoy. His mouth was warm and firm and as he held her close, the touch of his skin against her sent ripples of feeling along her body. She tried to pull away but he simply cradled her closer, his voice murmuring deep husky words of admiration in her ear.

'Come on now, this is what you set out to do. It was a very pretty display, my sweet one. I give you top marks for your initiative and your acting ability. If I hadn't seen you at the airport I would have thought you a mermaid under my window.' His blue eyes teased her. 'But no mermaid I know would get into a pool quite so slowly. You can't pretend to be a cold creature.'

His mouth teased hers for a moment, then descended firmly, masterful and direct. After the gentleness of his touch it was like a hot knife searing her, opening her petal-like mouth, crushing and demanding. Anna tried to fight, but it was awkward pushing him away one handed and holding her bikini top with the other! He had out-manoeuvred her completely. She felt response rushing through her like a set of drums played by a deft drummer.

'You have very kissable lips, long legs.' His eyes were amused but held a hint of passion. 'I find you very, very attractive.'

Anna hastily tied her bikini. She struggled to her feet but the man simply stood up, his smile mocking.

'Ah! More of the untouched routine. I suppose I'll play along. You're going to tell me that you thought yourself quite alone, that you had the place to yourself, right? Come on, golden legs, tell the truth, then we can both relax and enjoy ourselves.'

His eyes crinkled into a smile and the tan creases on his forehead bit deeper. Anna grabbed her towel and she looked at him with anger.

'Look, whoever you are, as far as I'm concerned, I wasn't expecting anyone and I don't know you!'

The man put his sinewy arms across his chest and surveyed her thoughtfully.

'Rather hackneyed, pet. I'm not the one who was doing the tempting, you were, remember? You made a good start, don't overdo it, I'm not feeling particularly energetic as it happens.'

'You conceited ape!' Anna was livid with rage. 'I wouldn't touch you if you paid me a million!'

CHAPTER TWO

THE man calmly stood there, his glance taking in every part of her from head to toe. Anna wrapped her towel around her, wishing it covered a little more.

'That's right, much more allure if there's something to uncover. You're a quick learner. What's your name, golden legs?'

'I wouldn't give you the time of day let alone my name,' she spoke wrathfully.

'Bravo! Just the right note of indignation, it sounded most effective, almost convincing. Now you think about your next move while I have my swim, I'm getting just a little bored.'

He left her swallowing her rage then dived into the pool, slicing through the water with his powerful, mahogany coloured arms and his dark head making brief appearances. He could swim well, noted Anna automatically, then furiously she turned and stomped off to the dressing room. She was aghast to find herself wondering just who was the wretched, conceited, arrogant man! His dismissal was the last straw. He was bored with her predictability!

Anna opened the door of the changing room and then looked at it puzzled. Only her shoes and her lingerie were neatly placed on the seat. She opened the room beside it but it was empty and she guessed that the wretch had removed her outer suit as a joke. She hesitated before trying

the back door of the house but it was securely
locked.

Anna wished she could have thrown the man
through the window. She dressed as much as she
was able then stamped back to the pool. The man
lay on his back, looking peaceful and totally
innocent.

'You think it's funny! Give me back my clothes
this minute!'

'Hush, were you not taught to say please?' He
spoke softly, but the edge in his voice ensured it
carried.

'Not when you removed them in the first place.
Now are you going to get them or . . .'

'Ah! Or what, I wonder?' His tone was slightly
interested.

Anna stamped her foot and her heel jarred on
the concrete.

'Temper, temper!'

He turned and began swimming leisurely
towards the end of the pool, then when she
thought he would climb out he turned and
expertly shot halfway down the pool. Anna
wished she could pour boiling oil over him but
the closest variety was her now forgotten suntan
lotion. Exasperated she returned to the house.
The upstairs window mocked her, the curtain
still floating softly in the breeze. It seemed to be
the only one open. A tree leaned over the side of
the house and she studied it. It was years since
she had climbed a tree but it looked relatively
easy.

A gleam shone in her eyes. If Mr Arrogant
expected to find her languishing for him on the
doorstep he would have to think again. She

dropped her towel and shoes reluctantly and hefted herself up to the first branch. The second and third were easy but the next was awkward and she edged out precariously before reaching it and swinging on to the roof.

She moved over it delicately as a cat and then dropped down to a flat section beside the window. To her relief it was a sliding one and she slipped it back and put one foot in, tentatively hoping that nothing was in the way. She was shaking when she sat on the bed a moment later, her feelings a kaleidoscope of rage, fear and relief. On the chair were her clothes and she began dressing hastily.

'Cup of tea or do you prefer champagne?' The voice called up the stairs. She gasped and shut the door. Looking around the room she saw the suitcases with their exotic labels and realised she was in the guest room. She combed her hair and pondered on the best course of action. At least she was dressed, she wasn't nearly so vulnerable as she had been in her bikini. The man would probably be waiting for her at the base of the stairs. She saw a radio and summoned up her courage. She would have the last laugh.

Opening the door, she called down, 'I'll have the tea please, with half a dozen cucumber sandwiches. I'm starving!'

'If it's available,' he called out. 'I see you discovered the front door was open'

She pulled a face. She hadn't thought to try that door, presuming it to be locked like the rear!

She turned on the radio. It blared into a song and she reopened the window, its clunk disguised by the music. Swiftly she eased herself through and along the roof, the journey much easier going down, then she grimaced as she caught her hand, scratching it on the tree in her hurry. Wincing, she clambered down the last branch and slipped into her shoes and picked up the handbag. Within seconds she had run along the lawn and down to the gate.

Heart pounding, she moved along the street, guessing that the radio would keep him fooled for a few moments. To her great relief a taxi was approaching. She hailed it and as it slowed down she gazed quickly back towards the house. She smiled, knowing she had won.

That smug, good looking man was about to fall flat on his face and she hoped he would land slap bang on his cucumber sandwiches!

But who was he? The question kept circling in her head as she climbed into the cab.

Anna gave her home address, she was far too shaken to return to the office and first she had to repair her dishevelled appearance. The taxi would cost her a fortune, she thought, as she examined her scratched hand. It was bleeding slightly and two of her manicured nails had broken. She grimaced, thinking that it was just as well Catherine Lester was away, she would have noticed them immediately. The thought made her sigh. Catherine had a guest with more than his share of masculine good looks and ego.

Only then did Anna realise she had left her bikini and her towel behind. It was mute evidence of her flight and she could just visualise the fun the man would have in hanging them from some post to humiliate her. Worse, he could hand them to Catherine and thereby find out her name, and present them himself! The thought that her boss was safely in the South Island gave her some comfort.

The luggage in the room had been untouched except for one small case, so he was probably only staying for a night before going about his business. She sighed, remembering her own work. She hadn't intended to be away so long and it would be another few minutes before she reached her flat in Ngaio then changed and caught a bus into the centre of town. The taxi driver let her off at the bank of architect designed apartments and she took out her key to unlock the door.

She showered, changed and glanced at her watch, it was almost three-thirty and she could just imagine some of the staff's comments about her privileged position. She put the last button through its hole and hastily changed the handbag for the matching one and ran to the door, slamming it behind her. With luck she would just make the bus.

Twenty-five minutes later she was sitting in her office looking at the notes the senior had handed her. One shook her slightly and she looked at the girl, anxiety shadowing her eyes.

'Mr Findlay rang at eleven and I was to call him on my return? He's in Wellington? Why on earth didn't you tell me when I dropped off the parcel or at least ring me at Mrs Lester's?'

'Sorry, Anna. I didn't see you after you'd dropped off Mrs Lester. Mr Findlay said that you could contact him at Mrs Lester's so I presumed you had met him and that's why you were so late back. I think he arrived back a day early and he intended to surprise his sister. I told him she had gone to Christchurch.'

'Well, he wasn't there so I guess there was no point in my ringing him.'

She opened her mouth and wondered if the man she had met was some business companion or overseas executive of Mark Findlay. He looked as if the world was his oyster and quite clearly he was used to girls falling pearl-like at his feet. Simply because he was so good looking with blue eyes and the way the dark curl hung little-boy-like over his forehead. And his kisses . . .

'I'm mad,' she muttered to herself. 'It's crazy to let some guy I'll never see again get under my skin.'

'Did Mr Findlay say that he was bringing back an overseas guest?' she asked the senior hopefully. 'He didn't ask for dinner to be reserved anywhere?'

'No, he just said that he would be sleeping most of the day then flying down to Christchurch.'

Anna thought rapidly. Mr Findlay could have met the mystery traveller and invited him. The company had a reputation for entertaining and hosting many important, overseas guests and Mrs Lester had several times looked after company contacts who had business in the capital.

But then there had been this crazy suggestion that Catherine had some interests in his love life. The man could be one of the single overseas agents, she decided. Catherine was a great believer in marriage. Anna could well imagine her boss playing the part of a matchmaker!

Anna stared at the 'phone with considerable

misgivings. While she had been sun-bathing and climbing in and out of windows, her boss had probably been snoring his head off a few rooms down the hall. If he had just flown for twelve hours from Tokyo then flown for another hour from Auckland to Wellington, he probably needed a rest. After all, he was about fifty or sixty, she remembered and even the most blasé traveller would be affected by jet lag. She could only hope he was not too angry by her apparent failure to disturb him.

She dialled the number keeping her fingers crossed that the man she met by the pool that day would not answer the 'phone. To her relief Mrs Lester's son answered.

'I was supposed to contact Mr Findlay. I was there earlier but I guess he was asleep.'

'Probably, Anna. Mum get away all right?'

'Yes, no problems. Are you the chief cook tonight or are you taking your uncle out?'

'No, he's cooking for us. You ought to see the video set he brought back for me, camera, tripod, the works. It's fabulous.'

'Wonderful, I'll look forward to seeing some of the movies you make with it.'

Privately she revised her opinion of Mr Findlay. He couldn't be all bad if he bought his nephew such a magnificent gift. She could only hope some of his nephew's pleasure had charmed him into accepting her long delay.

'Would you ask your uncle if he wants to speak to me?'

'Just a moment, Anna.' A minute later he was back. 'Anna? He said to tell you you're fired.'

'Oh, no!'

'Steady, I told him he can't do that to you, that you're really neat and Mum reckons you're the best secretary she ever had, so he says that he'll give you one more chance. Don't worry, Anna, I think he's joking.'

'I don't know that I'm going to like your uncle,' Anna said softly. 'Thanks for the good character reference.'

'Any time. I'll get you to help me with some of my video gear, Anna. Don't worry about Mark, he's beaut really.'

'I'll take your word for it,' Anna said soberly. It was all very well for Mark Findlay to utter threats about firing, but as far as she was concerned it wasn't funny. Carefully, she replaced the receiver, then realised that Mark Findlay had not wanted to speak to her about anything specific. Therefore, she reasoned, with growing anger, he had been merely checking up on her, to see if she was taking advantage of his sister's good nature!

He had rung at eleven and she must have missed his message at the airport by seconds and although she had returned to the office with the package she hadn't thought to check her desk, her thoughts had been on the swimming and the unexpected bonus of a couple of hours off. She grimaced as she realised that in Mark Findlay's eyes she had already earned the tag of inefficiency and stupidity and now he had apparently caught her being away from the office from eleven until almost four o'clock!

She didn't know how she was going to explain her lengthy absence to Mrs Lester. A tale of having to climb into her house across the rooftop to rescue her clothes sounded unbelievable. She must have wasted at least half an hour then, plus an hour going home to shower and change. The day she had been looking forward to so much had collapsed into an ugly mess.

Anna looked at the rest of the messages. It had been a busy time and one call from an agent was important. She began dialling the number immediately and dealt with the matter, then prepared letters for the next day. It was just six when she decided that she had done enough. The 'phone on her desk jangled and she answered it wondering who could be trying the office at that hour.

'Anna, thank goodness I've caught you. Listen my dear, I'm at my wits' end. The secretary the agency lined up for us is totally unsuitable. I want you to fly down here for a week or two until we can check out someone. It's all very awkward. Now my dear, I know I'm asking a lot but it will only be for a short period.'

'But I thought the agency . . .' Horror made her voice weak.

'Yes, the agency did everything we asked them to do. It's just that the person concerned is an old rival of Miss Penelope's. In the circumstances I think it would be foolhardy to have her living at the same house.

'I may be doing her an injustice but I don't want trouble. I'm afraid that I simply told the agency when they gave me her name that we had managed to find someone within the company. It was the only way out, that I could think of on the spur of the moment.'

Anna could tell her boss was very upset.

'Catch the same time flight that I took down this morning. Arrange for one of the staff to take your place for a short time. Would you believe my brother arrived a day early and is now in Wellington?'

'Yes, I know,' Anna supplied briefly.

'Fine, dear; you are a life-saver. I could only ask someone I relied on absolutely. I'll have one of the firm's cars meet you at the airport, in Christchurch. I'll tell them to park at the freight section, someone will be meeting the plane as it's the delivery one, so go straight to that area. Clear?'

'Yes,' Anna found herself saying, then frowned. Mrs Lester had taken it for granted that she would go and by saying yes she had implied that she would.

'Anna, this will be rather a good experience for you. My brother is very demanding but in the couple of weeks you are with him you'll learn more than I can teach you in the next six months. Learn this side and who knows, in a year or so's time you could become one of our agents. I'd be quite prepared to stake you for fifty per cent.'

Anna was flabbergasted. It was a staggering offer and she glowed at the possibility.

'That's very generous.'

'I know a good investment when I see one. However keep it to yourself and when you return, we'll discuss it further. After a short time with Mark you'll be quite capable. The more I think about it, the more I like the idea. Mark has to agree, so make a good impression on him and you're on a winner.'

The rosy dream of herself sitting in an

executive suite collapsed in a puff of wind. There was no way she could impress Mark Findlay. Unless, she rallied at the thought, she made an excellent job of being his secretary, for the next two weeks.

'Now, what business went on today? Anything special?'

Anna gave the details then told her that she had taken off longer than she had intended that afternoon and as she expected Mrs Lester wasn't concerned. Simply by being at the office at six Anna had more than made up for her earlier absence. Not that Mark Findlay would hear about that, she guessed wryly.

Anna caught the bus home and made a quick meal for herself. She was surprised to find that she was not in the least hungry, evidently the thought of having to work for Mark Findlay had removed all her appetite.

She rang through for her flight reservation with a great deal of misgiving and was disappointed that she was booked on immediately. For once the thought of going to the South Island did not appeal.

The large silver aeroplane with its distinctive Air New Zealand logo of a koru waited on the tarmac. The symbol of the palm leaf frond had been taken from the Maori, who had carved it on their giant canoes. Canoes that had carried their warriors to war as well as to exploration. She stepped on board certain in her mind that she was heading for war and she felt most unlike a warrior, armed only with her shorthand pen. The victims of many of those early wars had been eaten by the victor or kept prisoner as slaves. It was not a comfortable analogy.

A smiling hostess greeted her and pointed out her seat. Anna's eyes stared disbelievingly at the man who sat beside it, already busy with a sheaf of papers. Sensing her regard he turned enquiringly and she had the satisfaction of seeing his eyes widen.

'Oh well done! First time any girl's managed to find out my seat number. You really did make an effort, didn't you? After your surprise exit yesterday I wondered when I'd meet you again. Seeing you've been so imaginative I'll reward you with my whole attention for half this flight, fair enough?'

'Is there a problem?'

The hostess's query as she approached made Anna realise that she was holding up the queue. She sank down with a murmured apology and glared at the man.

'Look, I want to say two things. One, I don't know you from Adam; two, I didn't arrange to have this seat.'

'Long legs, you're far too pretty to bother with excuses. Allow me.'

He bent over her and fastened her seat belt and the touch of his hands sent a pulse soaring. It was echoed by the roar of the engines and she leaned back in her seat her fingers clenching on the edge of the seat. Flying, she told herself, was very safe, but telling herself that scarcely helped. She closed her eyes, instinctively keeping her head straight in front of her.

'Why, my poor little darling, you're petrified. Relax, just think, if we go we'll go together.'

'Thanks,' she muttered. 'You're a great help.'

The plane rolled out on the runway. She trembled as it turned, ready for its run down the tarmac. She was surprised to find her hand taken in sympathy and she found it oddly comforting. It seemed ages as the engines were tested again then the plane moved forward. She clenched her hand aware that her fingers were tightening in his in desperation but unable to think past the moment when the plane would leave the ground.

Suddenly she was aware of her head being held gently and his mouth taking hers. She tried to pull away but the firm seat held her immobile as the man captured her fear and removed it, smoothing it away with his experienced touch. Her eyes flew open meeting the dark blue of his gaze.

'See, my pet, you're still safe and we left Wellington behind some moments ago.'

Disbelievingly she looked for herself, peeping past him to see the green of the sea and the approach of the South Island. They were still climbing but already the hostess was handing out magazines.

'You know I'm wondering if I could have made a mistake. No-one who is so terrified of flying would deliberately seek such a meeting place.' He paused and looked at her consideringly. 'In which case I have to apologise and say that I've not only egg on my face, but cucumber as well!'

'I can't see it but I'll accept the apology,' said Anna a shade nervously.

The ruthless gaze which swept over her caused her to start feeling anxious but it was nothing to do with the plane. He picked up her hand and examined the fingers closely.

'No rings but plenty of scratches. Odd!'

'Not if you climb up trees and down again in order to get away from some male! I broke two nails,' she said accusingly.

'And lost your bikini.'

'That too! I only hope Mrs Lester doesn't start asking me about it.'

'Is she such a tyrant?'

'No, she's lovely, a super person.'

'What were you doing at the Lesters?'

'I took Mrs Lester to the airport and then had to return the car. Catherine suggested I enjoy the pool while I was there. I thought I was alone, I didn't know that her brother was there and had invited a guest.'

'You're almost convincing me,' he said slowly. He studied her face. 'You have lovely eyes, they remind me of clear streams, Anna.'

'How did you know my name?' Anna asked a shade breathlessly. The man had given it a soft inflection so it seemed quite unlike her prosaic name. Instead it became rather exotic and sensuous.

'Your ticket. It had your name and address in Wellington.' He handed it back with a lightning smile. 'You dropped it when we were taking off.'

She took it from him, thinking sourly that he didn't miss a trick.

'Look, Mr Whoever-you-are, I've no desire to see you again so just forget my name and address. Now why don't you study your papers. I'm sure you were doing something constructive before.'

'Beauty and sensibility. An intriguing combination! I'll take your advice.'

He proceeded to immerse himself in the papers

and Anna found herself totally ignored. She wondered what it was that held his attention so closely. From time to time he made a note in the document margins then made calculations on the tiny, almost flat calculator he pulled from his pocket.

Anna gradually became more and more irritated. It seemed as though she had failed or bored him in some way. She tried staring past him at the vista of snowy mountains below her, but he shifted his papers and she guessed that he was preventing her prying eyes from seeing what he was assessing. She gritted her teeth and pointedly looked in the opposite direction. The angle of the plane told her they were making their descent and the notice to fasten seat belts lit up. She fastened her own and realised that he had not noticed the sign. As the hostesses walked down the aisle he reached for it mechanically his eyes scarcely leaving his papers. Anna wondered why she was surprised. She remembered one of the first things she noticed about him was his look of an international traveller.

The plane banked sharply and she saw the curve of the sea edging the shore and the city of Christchurch spread out below. Calmly the man gathered up his papers then turned to look at her.

'How long are you in Christchurch, Anna?'

'About one or two weeks, I'm not sure.'

'Depends on the boyfriend, does it? Tell him from me he shouldn't leave you alone for too long.'

'You are presuming again,' said Anna icily.

He took her hand and kissed the scratches softly. 'I'm sorry.'

Anna pulled her hand away.

'Look, can't you get the message. I'm not interested, I think you are a walking disaster.'

'Anna, Anna, you don't mean that.'

The worst of it was, she knew in her heart she didn't. The wretch had so much attraction, so much sheer, male magnetism. It was just as well she was immune.

'Do you know the Christchurch area at all?'

'I've been there once or twice,' she conceded stiffly. 'About ten years ago.'

'Then you'll have to let me show you some of the tourist spots. What about meeting me tomorrow? Where are you staying?'

'I'm staying in the country and I shall not be available. I'm working.' She wished she hadn't added the explanation. His eyes flickered over her.

'So, you'll be entitled to some time off.' There was a dancing gleam in his eyes.

'Look, I'm going to work for an aged gentleman who keeps weird hours as most of his business is done in different time zones. He's a proper old termagent and a crackpot on efficiency and I'm not looking forward to the experience at all.'

'Why do it then?' he asked casually.

'Because I couldn't refuse. It is part of the same outfit, my boss in Wellington deals with the New Zealand side, the other is international.'

'Intriguing, tell me more.'

'It is fascinating. Dealing . . .' she stopped herself short from telling him about the cherished thought of one day having her own agency. One of the first rules was never to discuss business with others. '. . . in all sorts of lines,' she finished. She opened her bag and put away her ticket. She would need it for her return journey.

'Have you met this old buffer before?' He grinned at her sympathetically.

'No, just spoken to him on the 'phone.' She pulled an expressive face. 'It was not a pleasant experience for me.'

'It may not have been for him.'

'It was. I'm sure he gloated over catching me out. He sounds like a big, fat octopus sitting ready to pounce.' She raised her hands, spread her fingers and did a swift mimic of a waving octopus writhing and crushing a poor victim.

He laughed and his blue eyes were like sunlight on water.

'Do you know your stupid prank yesterday almost got me fired? I intended to be back at the office around two; thanks to your tomfoolery I had to spend a fortune on a taxi to go home, shower and change. By the time I got back it was almost four o'clock,' she finished belligerently. 'And it wasn't pleasant to find that the big boss had rung for me at eleven. As it was, I was there till after six, doing work I should have done earlier.'

She stood up as the plane rolled to a stop and realised that she had been so busy telling him what she thought of his actions that the plane had landed and she hadn't even thought about being scared.

'Let me make it up to you. Tomorrow night. I'll stand you dinner at the Camelot Room and don't worry about your boss—I'll straighten things out with him.'

'No thank-you. I told you. I have to exist with this creature for possibly two weeks, I don't want him upset. Nor do I feel any fascination for your oh-so irresistible presence,' she said with a note of sarcasm.

'Is someone meeting you?' he asked, ignoring her remark.

'Yes, I believe so.'

'We'll meet again, Anna.'

'Not if I can help it.'

He smiled down at her, a slow, sensuous, caressing smile that she recognised as a challenge. It made nonsense of her flippant words.

'I don't believe you'll be able to avoid me. Shall we see if I'm right?' he murmured.

Anna nodded, unable to speak. Despite her earlier denial she could only hope that he was correct!

CHAPTER THREE

A BREEZE was lifting Anna's hair as she stepped down from the plane and walked to the concourse area of the airport. The building itself was impressive and she looked around her, following the raggle taggle of travellers entering the gates. She found her way to the luggage section and collected her suitcases then carried them towards the freight section.

There was no sign of her mystery traveller and she wished she had asked his name. His suggestion for dinner had been tempting, she knew that Catherine Lester liked to go to the Camelot Room on her trips to Christchurch. Fleetingly she wished that she had taken him up on his offer, he was a very attractive man. She remembered that he had told her he would fix it with her boss. She frowned, sure that she had not been so indiscreet as to mention his name. Only then did she recall he had been staying in the same house at the same time and kicked herself for her heartfelt description of Mark Findlay. No wonder he had laughed. She could only hope that he would not relay the incident.

'Miss Anna Heathley?'

She looked at the man sent to meet her. He was a grey-bearded figure and she held out her hand wondering if he could be Mr Mark Findlay. He looked far too approachable, she decided.

'Catherine said to look after you, so any

problems come and see me. I'm John Carter. I work at the house with my wife, Sally. I'll take those bags for you; Carter by name, see?'

'Thank you very much.' Anna smiled, liking him immediately. 'Has Mrs Lester returned?'

'Not yet, she's at the local office, she wanted to see Mark first. He came down on your flight. I hope I didn't keep you waiting. I had to see him.'

'Not at all,' Anna said truthfully. 'There was a slight delay before I collected my luggage. I suppose you've known Mr Findlay a long time?'

'More than thirty years. I started work at "Orakau" when I was a lad. I helped lay out the golf course and just stayed on.'

'There's a golf course in the grounds?' asked Anna, wide-eyed. 'I've never even played.'

'You'll soon learn. It's not a bad, little course. Nine holes, but a good range of shots, the smallest is a hundred and ten and the longest four hundred and forty metres.' He seemed very pleased with the information but to Anna he was talking in meaningless numbers.

'I knew there were beautiful grounds around the house.'

'Oh, it's a showpiece all right. But the golf course is quite a feature; quite a few of the locals use it. Some of them think they own it.'

He swung the big car around a corner and grinned at her. 'But as a staff member you can use it any time. There is the swimming pool, too, just outside the office, another advantage of being in the country. If you want to go into town any time just check with Mark or with my wife or I. There's usually transport going or you might get

the use of one of the cars. I should have asked
Catherine about it.'

'It's all right, I can probably catch a bus or a
taxi.'

The man laughed as though she had said
something funny and she joined in after a quick
glance around, realising they had left the town
behind. The Canterbury Plains surrounded them
and they headed towards the hills passing the
occasional cluster of houses and stores. Trees
broke the horizontal viewpoint their vertical
strength giving a balance to the eye.

Again they turned and Anna checked the
signpost.

'Only another five minutes,' John Carter told her.

Suddenly all her fears crowded in on her. The
place sounded magnificent, more like a palace
than an office and she knew she didn't have to
look far for the snag.

'Can you tell me a little about Mr Findlay,' she
enquired hesitantly.

'Mark? One of the best! Looks after his staff;
mind you, he can't stand shirkers or gossips.
They wouldn't last two minutes with him. Once
he knows you can do a job he leaves you to get on
with it. It won't be easy stepping into Miss
Penelope's shoes. She's been used to his way of
working and even she says he's always like a bear
with a sore head after one of his international
flights. We always try to stay out of his way for a
day or two until he's caught up with some sleep.
Trouble is, he always wants to inspect everything
the minute he returns.'

He grinned conspiratorily and tapped the side
of his nose in a knowing gesture.

'Take my tip. Try to persuade him to get to bed early the first couple of nights and then he'll be as good as gold. You're in luck, at least he's had twenty-four hours in Wellington, so he would have caught up with some sleep there.'

He paused and turned down a narrow road.

'I know Miss Penelope liked to have the telex stuff laid out for him and all the urgent lists but apart from that I can't help you. Do you know everything else?'

'Some, I guess I ... Oh look, isn't that magnificent, the house on the rise.'

She looked at it in delight. Trees and park-like lawns created a jewel-like setting for the large homestead. In front she could see a golf course and as she watched two women sauntered along, pushing their trundlers full of gear.

'That's home,' John Carter beamed proudly. 'See the golf course?'

'It looks beautiful!' She guessed that the course was his pride. She remembered the photo Catherine Lester had shown her and knew that it must have been taken from round the side. As the big car swept up to the pillared entrance she felt grateful that her arrival had preceded Mr Findlay. At least she would have time to get her things unpacked, she hoped.

'Welcome to Orakau. Here's my wife, Sally, to meet you.'

A diminutive figure smiled at her and Anna relaxed thinking that both John and Sally Carter looked good-natured. A moment later she was shown around by Sally.

'The office is just there.' Sally pointed to a forbidding, deep, oak door. 'Mark's suite is next to it. On the other side there's the entrance to Miss Penelope's flat. Here we are, Catherine's given you her own suite. It's rather pretty, I'm sure you'll like it.'

Anna followed her in and stood impressed. The room had been designed with Catherine Lester in mind. It was elegant and feminine in tones of blue and deep sapphire blue. A silver dressing table set and silver fittings formed a contrast. The sunlight pouring into the room relieved the colour that would otherwise have made it too cold.

'Now I'll put the kettle on and start making some lunch while you explore, you'll find your bathroom through there, and the lounge.'

Weakly Anna nodded. Her eyes took in the bank of wardrobes along one wall and she followed through the arch to a dressing area adjoining a bathroom with a shower, toilet and vanity unit in blue and silver. Rich, velvety sapphire blue towels with a matching flannel were left on the silver towel rail. Through the next arch was another sunfilled room, again with the pale blue washed background but the lounge suite was covered in blue, purple and pink design linen. Cushions in pink relieved the colour and a large watercolour of a cherry blossom tree picked out the same tones.

Anna put some of her clothes on to the hangers in the wardrobe. Later, she would have plenty of time for looking around, first she had to get her bearings on the office before her tough boss arrived. She grinned at her anxious reflection and sped down the corridor. A friendly tinkle of crockery reminded her that she was hungry and she wondered if she dared take time to eat.

Looking at her plate a moment later she realised that Sally Carter was a superb cook. The salad on her plate was crisply fresh and the twist of orange and grapefruit set it off.

'Relax, dear. You're looking as though the big, bad wolf is about to pounce on you. I'm not expecting Mark back for a couple of hours. Catherine was leaving on the two o'clock flight so he won't be home before that. The office will let me know, they generally ring when he leaves, so I can have a drink organised for him the minute he walks in.'

'What a good idea! I can enjoy this.'

Reassured, Anna soon cleared her plate and had two cups of tea before returning to her unpacking. Once done, she put away the suitcases neatly, then satisfied walked along to the office.

The oak door yielded softly at her touch and she stepped into a richly carpeted area with an enormous desk. An excellent typewriter lay covered on top. Empty trays revealed nothing as she opened the door leading out of the office to find a large room with another desk of a similar size. In one corner a computer flicked up coded information. For a minute she watched it and knew that it was exactly the counterpart of the one she had worked with in Wellington.

Automatically her eyes decoded and translated it as it flickered and she sat and typed in her requests for the day's readings. A few seconds later the information was being put on to type and she notated it automatically. She noticed one line was considerably higher than usual and she

set her memory to work, then sought confirma-
tion. As she had suspected it had firmed
considerably and she laid the information on the
big desk.

She hesitated, wondering if Mr Findlay would
consider it presumptuous of her. Catherine was
always pleased to have some of the work done for
her but that didn't mean her brother would feel the
same. No doubt he would soon tell her! He would
probably be more interested in her filing ability.

Reminded, she studied the system and soon
found it was in two sections; one local, the other
international. It took her only minutes to realise
the local system was familiar, most of the clients
she had dealt with in the past six months as
Catherine's secretary. The international one was
the one she had to master but the sheer size of it
and the interlinking of many of the companies
told her it would be no easy task. It took her
some moments to realise the colour codings gave
a clue to the networks as well as the computer
programmes.

To confirm it she tried a programme and
within seconds the past dealings with the London
office flickered on the screen. Fascinated she
began tapping in questions, learning a little of the
way Mark Findlay worked. No wonder, she
decided, that there was such a pile of mail waiting
for him.

'Anna?' Sally's sparrow bright eyes smiled.
'My goodness, you'll give that computer stomach
ache the way your fingers are flying. Have a
rest while you've got the chance. The other office
just rang and told me Mark's gone out to the
airport with Catherine so you've got a bit longer.'

Anna switched off the programme and replaced it. 'I do feel a bit jaded,' she admitted. 'There's an awful lot to learn.'

'Why don't you have a swim? Mark thinks it's the best tonic.'

'Marvellous idea. I will.'

Within minutes she was in a modest, one piece suit she had put in her case. She could allow herself twenty minutes, she decided, remembering how long it had taken them to travel from the airport to home. That would still allow her a further twenty minutes time to dress before the big, bad wolf arrived.

She swam up and down the pool, the touch of the water silky on her skin. After the tension of the flight and the worry over the work, she felt a great relief. Surely it wouldn't be too hard living and working with Mrs Lester's brother? Besides, she reminded herself, it was only for a week or possibly two. Catherine Lester had promised her a replacement after that time.

She cut through the water neatly then did a duck dive under the pool in sheer exuberance before spluttering her way to the surface. She repeated the manoeuvre several times then swam contentedly up and down the pool, before lying lazily, letting the water float her. She knew she should get out but it was tempting to stay a little longer. A float mattress lay on the side and she decided to try it for a few minutes. The sun nursed her limbs as she floated, pushed along by the merest slow kick or twist of her wrist.

A splash beside her made her open her eyes. She sat up in astonishment and, thus disturbing the balance, promptly fell off as the mattress tipped. Spluttering and treading water she looked at the new swimmer in surprise.

'What are you doing here?' she asked indignantly.

He smiled with a hint of relish. 'I live here. Call me Mark. Mark Findlay!'

Horror overcame her. 'But you can't be! You're not old!' she ended with a wail.

'Age is relative; now those trees over there were planted on my first birthday. That was thirty-four years ago, hopefully the trees will be around in a couple of hundred years time, which makes them mere "babes in wood".' He grinned, his eyes telling her that he was enjoying her discomfort.

'Mrs Lester always refers to you as her "big" brother.'

'I grew taller than Catherine when I was fourteen. Just a family joke. There's quite a gap between us. Now you would be about twenty-five, correct?'

'Yes.' There was little point in denying her age. It would be easy enough for him to check it out in the file.

'Now I seem to remember you calling me . . . what was it? . . . ah yes, a weird old gentleman, a termagant, an efficiency crackpot, and a slimy, big, fat octopus.'

'I didn't say slimy,' Anna said weakly.

'Possibly not, but the impression was definitely there. I am going to enjoy having your company, Miss Heathley.'

'Your middle name wasn't Shylock, was it?' she countered swiftly.

'The pound of flesh? No, I don't think that's

necessary or desirable. I can think of lots of other suggestions which would please me far more. The first being your presence in the office in fifteen minutes.' Suddenly his voice had the crackle of authority. Anna turned wordlessly and climbed out of the pool.

Exactly fifteen minutes later she was in his office and seated at her desk, her heart still racing. His earlier discovery of her at the Lester's pool and his comments, began to make sense. Being a good-looking bachelor who seemed to have the Midas touch, he probably was constantly pursued. She pressed her lips firmly in disgust. She, Anna Heathley, was not going to join the race. She had suffered quite enough at the hands of a so-called 'eligible young man' and once was enough! Her eyes shadowed at the memory and she hastily sorted out her pens and checked her desk for stationery.

A moment later Mark Findlay strode in, his hair, still damp from his swim, curling tightly around his head. His eyes glanced round his domain for a moment with a definite air of satisfaction until they rested on her. Clearly she was a poor substitute for Miss Penelope.

'Right, I'll have the read-outs first.'

'On your desk, Mr Findlay,' she answered quietly.

'I said, call me Mark! I do not like repeating myself, clear?'

'Yes.' She left the name unsaid and it twanged all the more because she hadn't said it. He went into the inner office and Anna tried to remain mouse-like as she heard him pick up the papers.

'Anna?'

She took her notepad and entered the room. Before it was just a luxurious office, now the man seemed to fill it.

'Explain your analysis of this situation.' He pointed to the papers she had noted.

Nervously she licked her lips. The comfort of knowing her facts helped her.

'I believe we could be affected, as Mrs Lester had ordered a monthly amount. Our estimates were based on June prices with an overall allowance of ten per cent. The prices now are running above twelve per cent. We are still within our margins, the price was at seven per cent at the last increase, but if there is another jump we should be prepared to renegotiate or look at alternatives. I ran the options through earlier, but this still looks the best deal.'

'Good. I'll look at the files later. Let's have a look at the mail. There's bound to be some here. Take the imports first.'

His tone was brisk and businesslike. She made swift notes. Only two he held back for further study.

'Right, I'll have the files relevant for these two letters and their payment record. While I have a look at that, make a start on the replies and bring the first ten in as soon as you can.'

He glanced at his watch and Anna knew that he had done it with the idea that she wasn't to waste his time or hers. She bristled inwardly but, outwardly calm, fetched the files and put them on his desk.

It took her longer than normal to complete the ten letters. Every address she had to check as well as every computer number code. An hour later she was beginning to feel frayed at the edges. Apart from a cursory glance as she placed the letters with their notes on his desk, he ignored her. She was as much interest to him as the wallpaper on the office wall, she thought sourly. He would give her his attention when he wanted something, otherwise he had his work and she had hers. She told herself that was fine as far as she was concerned. Why, then, did she feel decidedly annoyed with Mark Findlay?

The tea Sally had brought in earlier was removed cold as she worked on, her mind fixed on the slowly, diminishing pile of letters in front of her.

Mark stood beside her and glanced at his watch and she could mentally feel his eyes running over the pile and his estimation of how long she had taken.

'That's fine for now. Take an hour off and report back here to me then.'

Silently she looked at him, then stood up and left the room. Somewhere a clock struck and she heard the chimes ring seven. Engrossed in her work she had no idea it was so late. No wonder she felt hungry, tired and irritated with Mark Findlay!

She went towards the kitchen and Sally Carter looked at her anxiously.

'Oh, you poor dear. Was it too bad? Now sit here, lovey and I'll put your dinner up.'

The warmth was tangible, like being wrapped in heated rugs after suffering a blizzard. Minutes later she was seated at the table and in front of her was an appetising meal. Sally Carter had prepared a similar one on a tray for Mark, she realised, as it was carried through.

'John and I had ours earlier. I was hoping that Mark would have taken things a little easier this time, but he's always the same. Likes to get everything back under control. He'll probably be up half the night, I shouldn't wonder. Miss Penelope would send him off to bed.'

Anna looked at the devoted Sally and managed a worn smile. 'Sorry, I can't imagine me telling him the same thing.'

She wandered round the darkening garden then re-entering the house checked her appearance in the hall mirror. When the hour was up she returned to the office. Mark Findlay was waiting for her.

'I've written out some memos I want typing out and made notes for the last two letters. I'm going off for a rest. I'll be back at eleven as I have to ring London. Just leave those letters for me to sign when you're finished. At the speed you typed the earlier lot you should have that done in no time! Goodnight.' His glance flickered over her briefly and she turned and went back to her desk.

'Crazy beast!' she muttered. 'I'm not super-woman!'

She looked at the pile and knew that she would be lucky to have done them before he returned at eleven o'clock. Clearly he had his own way of getting back at her for calling him a crackpot on efficiency.

By the time ten o'clock came she felt as though lead weights were tied to her eyes. She piled up the work she had done and put it on his desk.

There was no point in carrying on, she would have to retype the last two memos. If Mark Findlay wanted to complain he would have to haul her out of bed to do it! There were still more waiting but she would do them much faster the next day.

The blue room was restful and relaxing and she climbed into bed, too tired to do more than close her eyes. Never had a day seemed so long and the many sides of her boss were more puzzling than ever.

It was ten o'clock before the sunlight pouring into her room woke her and she opened puzzled eyes at her strange surroundings. Memory made her sit up and look at her watch. Within minutes she was dressed and scurrying along the thick carpeting to Mark Findlay's office. Her heart was pounding, she could just imagine the lecture she would receive. To her intense relief the office was empty. She sat down at her desk, switched on the typewriter and read the laconic message on her paper.

'Back at eleven.'

She wondered when he had written it. Five minutes before, an hour earlier? She looked at the remains of the pile from the previous night and began working through them. The clock was chiming as Mark Findlay walked into the room.

'You slept well.'

It was a dry statement as his eyes flicked over her.

'Yes, thank you. I'm sorry I slept in. It won't happen again.'

He said nothing, but his glance was annihilating.

'I've completed these memos you wanted last night. It wasn't any use me doing them after ten, I was too tired,' she explained.

'What were you doing working till that time? There was no need for that. I don't appreciate martyrs,' he said sardonically.

Anna snapped the pencil she was holding, in her anger. The wretch had told her distinctly to leave the work on his desk.

'Now that you are here I'll sign them and perhaps then we can make a start on today's mail.'

Anna obediently gave him the sheaf, then hastily opened the mail. She was still sorting it through when he signalled her. Twenty minutes later she was back at her desk thinking that the man certainly knew precisely what he was doing. His grip on the accounts and the legal aspect was impressive, until she remembered that he had done both professionally. It made him hard to live up to, she decided, as she inserted another paper in her machine. It was lunch time before she was finished and was dismissed with a wave. She was just finishing her light salad when he entered the room and sat beside her.

'You can send that pile away and this afternoon I want a copy of the changes to the customs regulations. When you've done that you can take time off. Book a table for two at the Camelot room and be ready to go out at seven-thirty.' His eyes took in her business suit, a severe deep blue linen. 'Wear something to match that curl.'

He smiled and turned his attention to the salad. Anna gritted her teeth and instinctively her hand flew to the offending curl. He had invited her out to that particular restaurant while he was on the plane, she remembered.

'Yes?'

He looked at her in surprise because she was still standing in front of him. The lettuce stayed on his fork and she wished it would fall, she knew it would have done if the positions had been reversed.

'I'm sorry, I don't like mixing business with pleasure.'

He looked at her quizzically.

'You do it for business then. I'll do it for pleasure. If the acting head can take you out for a meal, then the head certainly can. The precedent has been set.'

Fuming, Anna turned and walked back to her office. She finished the work he had required then hesitated, her hand on the telephone book. If it had been Catherine Lester who had invited her she would have been excitedly planning what to wear for the occasion, but her brother was a different proposition.

She wondered if once away from the office he would revert to the playboy image he had shown by the pool and on the plane. Her lips tingled and she stood up, irritated with her own emotions. She was not going to go with him. He was far too dangerous when his eyes rested on her lips and his hand held hers and his voice whispered that she had kissable lips.

Anna thumped the telephone book down on the table. She would go but she would make it very obvious that she was to be looked at and not touched! Swimming in the pool, Anna gradually cooled down. She could hear the computer clicking and the occasional 'phone ringing, but she ignored it. He had told her to take the time off and she would. It certainly made up for the hours she had worked the day before. Mentally she reviewed her wardrobe. She had one frock with her which was suitable for most occasions, a neat, demure, grey silk with a tiny, russet print. It looked drab until she put it on when it seemed to swirl into place with a smugness of fit which made it almost mischievous. It had always been one of her favourites and she knew that she could carry off the unusual colouring; the brown highlighting her hair and her brown eyes.

Dressed that evening she checked her appearance, straightening the small gold pendant and the gold chain around her wrist. With a final touch of perfume for luck she left the room and walked down the passage. She looked up and saw the tall, dark man standing outside the office. She wondered fleetingly what Mary, Queen of Scots, had felt like as she walked along to meet her fate.

Mark looked at her and a smile curved his mouth.

'Sexy, yet elegant. I approve.'

She answered waspishly, wanting him to clearly understand how she felt. 'Just don't handle the merchandise.'

'If you break me, consider me sold?' His eyes teased her.

He led the way to the limousine and carefully closed the door after her. Quickly she fastened the seat belt, she was going to give him no excuse to touch her. The car's luxury cushioned her and she leaned back appreciatively.

His grip on the wheel was firm yet at ease. He

drove well, she conceded, as they pulled up outside the turreted hotel.

'Seeing you are only here for a short time you should enjoy some of our fine, modern architecture. Remind me to take you to the Town Hall,' he said blandly, as he took her arm. He led the way through the impressive entrance then followed along the small corridor to a tastefully appointed bar.

'This is one of my favourite places, The Den of the Red Fox. What would you like to drink? Don't suggest tea and cucumber sandwiches!'

Anna glanced around. The curved booths with their buttoned red velvet upholstery were not only comfortable, but also gave a great deal of privacy.

'I'll have a dry sherry, please,' she said, as he stood waiting for her order. Her glance was caught by the stained glass window featuring a little red fox. Its bright eyes were shrewd and reminded her more than a little of her host.

'Good health!' he toasted her a moment later. She acknowledged his gesture and raised her own glass.

'To merchandising.'

He smiled swiftly and Anna felt her heart race. He had a lovely smile, she noticed, his blue eyes sparkled and the dark curls which persisted in hanging down his forehead seemed to join in. His smile seemed to warm her, spreading a glow from her mouth to her toes. She looked down at her sherry. Surely one small drink could not make her see Mark Findlay in such an attractive light?

CHAPTER FOUR

ANNA was aware of Mark looking away and his attention held by a new couple who had just walked in. Automatically Anna looked at the girl. She was beautiful, dainty and petite, her black hair swept into a topknot, her eyes dark and her lips pouting as she turned to look at her escort.

Anna felt herself go rigid, recognising the man immediately. Maurice Caswell had been the man of her dreams for so long it seemed strange to actually see him. He did not notice her. He looked as handsome as ever and the intervening four years seemed to have left no mark on him. A trick of fate had brought her within a few feet of the man who had almost wrecked her life. She licked her lips as the astringency of the sherry settled on her mouth.

'Do that again and I'll kiss you.'

Wide-eyed, she looked at Mark, his vibrancy shocking her back to the present. She stared at him for a moment then found herself smiling at him in delight. For years, she had dreaded being in the same room with Maurice Caswell, certain that she would become a fountain of tears or something equally disastrous, yet now that it had happened, she felt nothing. She had been surprised, but that was all. Long emotions she thought she would never forget had disappeared and she almost laughed at the discovery.

She was free, totally, gloriously free!

'I think I'd better get you to our table, clearly you are feeling like climbing Mount Cook. One sherry and you're floating.'

Anna hugged her secret and smiled sweetly at the big, bad beast.

'If you like!'

She knew he looked at her sharply and she struggled to put on a more sedate expression, but her smile kept popping out like sparkles in a champagne bottle. Even Mark wasn't going to spoil the evening.

Once seated in the giant room she gazed around her with interest, noting the heavy beams and the high ceilings, the suits of armour and the crests all contributing to the atmosphere. A fire burned brightly in a cauldron-like hanging, the flames echoed in the glasses and fine napery.

'It is beautiful,' she said happily.

'So are you,' Mark Findlay said quietly. 'You remind me of a Christmas tree; before you were beautiful but now it's as if someone has switched the lights on and you're glowing.'

Her eyes went to his and she felt her heart pound at the expression in them. She was astonished at his perception.

'Thank you,' she said softly.

He ordered, consulting her wishes and then suggested they dance while they were waiting. The music was unashamedly sentimental and the singer gave full justice to the number. She slipped into Mark's arms, feeling them holding her and thoroughly enjoying the experience. It was amazing, she told herself, what a difference seeing Maurice had made. She wished she had seen him years earlier. She had wasted four years.

The freedom gave her the mischievousness to snuggle closer to Mark Findlay, in sheer gratitude, her eyes peeping up at him.

'And you told me not to touch the merchandise,' he whispered as they drew to a halt.

'Well, well, well! It's amazing the people you run into!' The hearty voice made them both look up. 'Anna, you look enchanting. Mark, back from your travels? Conquered more worlds?'

Maurice Caswell turned to the diminutive figure by his side.

'Darling, I know you're an old friend of Mark's, but I don't think you ever met Anna. My wife Clare, Anna Heathley.'

'How do you do?' The formal phrase was useful at last, thought Anna.

'Maurice, would you and your wife join us?'

'Delighted, wouldn't we darling?'

Anna was sorry Mark had invited the couple. She supposed it would give her time to hear how his wife was wonderful and his children magnificent, she thought with a naughty chuckle. And, of course, it meant that she would not be alone with Mark, which was a good thing, wasn't it?

Their table was rapidly rearranged and Mark ordered champagne.

'Let's drink a toast to sweethearts,' he said as the steward poured the wine.

Anna looked at him sharply, wondering how he had guessed at the former relationship.

Then she saw his gaze was on Clare Caswell and her heart almost stopped. He hadn't been thinking of his secretary at all but the petite, pouting beauty who sat beside him. While their first course was served Maurice Caswell danced with his wife. With her interest in her food suddenly lost Anna felt inexplicably deflated. Mark was uncaring, his glance dark as he followed the couple on the floor.

'So, tell me about Maurice and your relationship.'

She spoke casually. 'I knew him once, a long time ago. There's nothing to it.'

'And roosters lay eggs! You saw him in the Den and that's when you lit up. When did you see him last?'

'Four years and three months ago.' As soon as she had spoken she wished she hadn't been so accurate.

'That would be just before his wedding,' Mark said thoughtfully. 'You're better off without him, he's a philanderer,' he said brutally. 'I didn't think he would marry Clare, but he needed her money, he was almost broke by then.'

Anna knew the reason. At the time it had caused her pain.

'I don't think you should judge him. I'm sure he loves her.'

'Grow up, Anna! When are you going to admit he doesn't love anyone but himself.'

'That's a lousy thing to say,' she said quickly. 'If that's the way you feel why did you invite them to share our table?'

'So I could keep a watch on the situation. Clare's an old friend of the family.'

'Don't worry. I won't seduce him under your nose,' Anna flung at him crossly.

'I'll make sure that you don't,' he answered calmly.

She glared at him and was almost pleased when

the couple returned and Maurice asked her to dance. Deliberately she ignored the slight hint of warning in the glance Mark shot her. She would flirt outrageously just to annoy him.

'I'd love to dance.' She smiled at Maurice and the band struck up a familiar melody. 'Goodness me, a tango! I doubt if I can still remember how it goes.'

'I asked for it especially, darling. How could I forget? You always were a wonderful dancer.'

Expertly he guided her and Anna began enjoying the dance her feet flying, instinctively matching Maurice's so that it was almost like an exhibition. When the band changed the music at the end, to a more slow, sentimental ballad, her breathing was rapid and her cheeks flushed.

'Oh Anna!' whispered Maurice. 'Anna, I've missed you. Look we still match, just like peaches and cream. That dance was marvellous. I'd forgotten what fun we used to have and how wonderful it was just to be together.'

'Some things it's better to forget,' said Anna, easing herself away from his grip, all thoughts of flirtation gone. 'Don't forget you're married.'

'Anna, don't spoil it. Just let me hold you. You're so beautiful Anna, so graceful, so elegant.'

He looked at her and Anna decided that his earnest attentions had not changed. Before she had revelled in every compliment, now she knew it was just part of his make-up.

'Your wife is very pretty, Maurice.'

'Anna, darling, let's just forget everyone else. I'm dreaming. I was wrong. This is how it should have been, the two of us together.'

'But it isn't and I've no desire to change.'

His lack of loyalty appalled her. She sought to change the subject.

'Have you children?'

'Yes. One boy and one girl. Clare believes in doing things correctly.' His tone was eloquent.

'I don't think you should make comments like that,' said Anna gently.

'Well, who else can I tell if not the one woman I've always loved? My mistake was in not realising how impossible it would be to forget you. Anna, I'm not letting you go, not now you've come into my life again.' He pulled her closer, as though the action would confirm the words.

'Maurice, until a few minutes ago you hadn't thought of me for years. I think we'd better return to the table.'

To make sure, she stopped dancing and turned in the direction of Clare and Mark. Immediately she wished she hadn't. Mark was looking at her as if he was considering which part he would slice off first. Clearly he believed that she had been encouraging Maurice. The arrival of the waiter helped ease the tension. On the surface all was bright, bubbling conversation but underneath there was a stream of undercurrents.

When they had completed their meal Clare turned to Mark.

'I'm afraid I'm not such a good dancer as Anna, but perhaps you'll dance with me for old friendship's sake, Mark?'

'I don't need a reason and you don't need an excuse,' he answered smoothly, rising nobly to the occasion. His hand as he reached for Clare's, rested on Anna's shoulder for a flash; she knew

his touch was a warning, a reminder that
although he was on the floor he would be
watching her.

Maurice turned to her eagerly the minute the
pair walked to the dance floor.

'Darling, where are you staying? When did you
come to Christchurch? There are a thousand
things I want to talk to you about.'

'I'm only here for a very short time. I'm
working for Mark,' she said. 'I'm a career girl
and my job means a lot to me,' she said
meaningfully.

'Rubbish! You would have given it all up for
me four years ago.' He was entirely confident.
Anna wondered how she could have been so
fascinated by him.

'That was a long time ago and my feelings
about work are quite different now.' She smiled.
'I suppose in a way it's thanks to you. I learnt
that work was one way to forget. Then I became
interested by the challenge of the job. An
executive secretary is a well paid post. I've my
own townhouse, I can afford overseas travel. Yes,
Maurice, I should say thank-you. Dumping me
for Clare was the best thing that could have
happened to me.'

'You've grown hard, Anna,' he said peevishly.
'You used to be soft and comforting.'

'You make me sound like a leftover marshmal-
low,' she laughed.

'Anna, you're so beautiful,' he said suddenly
leaning towards her, his voice urgent. 'I must talk
to you.' He picked up her hand and dropped a
kiss into her palm.

She drew her hand away slowly.

'My marriage is in ruins.'

He said the words quietly and for once Anna caught the genuine note of feeling in his voice. Sympathetically she looked towards him.

'Surely with your charm you can patch it up. What happened? Did Clare find you with someone else?' She saw the point had hit home.

'It wasn't like that,' he began. 'Well, yes, with you I have to be honest and admit it. It was just one of those things, it meant nothing.'

'It meant a great deal to your wife,' said Anna soberly. 'And possibly to the girl as well.'

'But Clare's threatening to dismiss me from the directorship. Without that I'd have no money.'

Anna shook her head. Maurice hadn't changed. He didn't care for his wife or the girl, he was only concerned that his punishment would affect him.

'Anna, I've always been able to talk to you,' he said urgently. 'Meet me, you'll be able to think of something.'

'Why not a marriage guidance counsellor?' Anna suggested.

'But darling Anna, they don't know me. You do, you've always understood me.' He leaned closer and gripped her hands tightly. 'Anna, I need you.'

He released her hands abruptly as Mark moved towards them. One glance at Mark's icy expression told Anna that he had heard Maurice's last urgent words.

'Your wife will return in a moment.' Mark's voice was clipped. Anna tensed, hearing the barely controlled anger in his tones. She could only be glad Clare had gone to the powder room and not heard Maurice's request.

'Anna, we're leaving.'

The order fell like a chunk of ice down Anna's spine. She pushed her chair back and stood with some attempt at dignity.

'I'm pleased to have met you and your wife, goodnight, Maurice.'

Her words seemed only to madden Mark. He gave her an annihilating glare and Anna knew that all the talking in the world would not convince Mark that he had misinterpreted Maurice's words.

She followed as he led the way to the car park. He ushered her into the car and then shut the door with just a trace more firmness than was necessary. The lights stabbed a path along the deserted streets then lit the corners of the roadside as the car moved powerfully towards Orakau. The silence held them apart, Anna conscious of every click of the dashboard clock.

Her throat was dry, it was impossible to swallow. The seat belt pinned her in place cutting tightly against her flesh. Nervous, her fingers fiddled futilely with the adjustment, trying to ignore the burning anger of the man, taut beside her.

He pulled up outside the main doors of Orakau. His hand moved to switch off the key. The engine died, making the silence more obvious.

'Thank you for an interesting evening,' Anna forced herself to speak.

'Is that what you call it? A useful diversion to fill the time.'

'That's unfair,' Anna protested. 'You put your own interpretation on a few words.'

'What other interpretation can I place on it?

He was holding your hand, murmuring sweet nothings. Let me guess? "Anna, you look beautiful, darling. I've made a mistake, it's you I want"!'

Mark enunciated each word clearly as he turned round in his seat. His dark, good looks seemed emphasised by the shadows cast by the light at the front door.

'Well, tell me I'm wrong!'

Weakly Anna shook her head. 'I didn't encourage him. It didn't mean . . .'

'Didn't encourage him? You all but flashed neon signs at him. Look at the way you danced together. You were begging him to make love to you.' He unsnapped her seat belt and the motion seemed to act as a trigger.

'Darling, I need you,' he mimicked Maurice cruelly. He moved, imprisoning her against the seat, one hand holding her head, the other at her waist. His mouth descended, demanding and brutal, forcing her lips to open. The kiss pulsed with their anger.

Anna's struggles only inflamed him, their attraction flaring like a blowtorch to ignite their passions. When he released her Anna was shaking and trembling, outraged as much by his action, as with her own response.

'At least Maurice Caswell's never forced himself on a woman!' she gasped.

His eyes glittered tiger-like and she thought he was going to strike her. Instead he drew a raw, long, slow, lung-filling breath and she could see him fight for control. He opened his door and swung himself out. Numbed, Anna watched as he strode round the car and opened her door.

'My apologies. You are not to involve yourself with Maurice Caswell while you are here. I'll see you in the office at eight-thirty.' His voice was cold.

Somehow she managed to get out of the car and walk up the steps. Behind her she heard Mark start the engine and a minute later the headlights washed over her as he turned the car towards the garage.

She stumbled as much with emotion as with the sudden, blinding light. Realisation followed her footsteps that with Mark the physical attraction between them was too great to be set aside. If her emotions had not been so primitive she would never have lost her dignity by insulting him so badly. From now on it would be war between them.

A bird trilling happily outside her window woke her. She stirred, wondering why she felt so heavy and despondent, then remembered the events of the night before.

She decided to be cool, efficient and capable. She would be the perfect secretary. Their relationship would be on a strictly business level.

The bird continued its paeans of trills and she smiled, thinking that she might as well see what was causing the bird so much joy. She opened the curtain a little and the sunlight flooded in. The outlook across the lawns to the trees was very beautiful. It was hot. Within a few yards was the pool, gloriously deserted; no-one else would have been woken by the bird with ambitions to turn into an alarm clock!

It took only a few minutes to change into her

swimsuit and grab another of the thick, soft
towels. She could have refreshing start to the day,
after all swimming was one of the more
rewarding aspects to the time she would spend
here. There was some compensation in working
for Mark Findlay!

. Eagerly she stepped out across the lawn and
entered the pool area. Immediately she saw
Mark, his dark head arrowing its way across the
pool, his powerful shoulders dipping in turn.
On reaching the end he flipped and swam just
as swiftly to the other end. She lost all desire to
swim. He was like an otter in the pool and she
had no intention of letting him place her at a
disadvantage. From his speed and straight lines
he was exercising and even a coach at the side
of the pool couldn't have found fault with his
smooth, sleek style. Disconsolately she walked
away, glad that he hadn't seen her standing
there.

Promptly at eight-thirty she entered the office.
Mark was seated at his desk, but his eyes flicked
over her.

'Good morning.'

Her voice was steady as she had practised in
her room before she had summoned all her
courage to face him . It was ridiculous, to be so
worried by a mere man. She was an adult, she
was good at her work and she didn't have to like
him or need his good opinion!

'Good morning,' he answered abstractedly, his
head already down bent as he studied a row of
figures. He made a note then looked up at her.

'I normally swim between six and seven each
day. You may join me if you choose. If you prefer

having the pool to yourself it is usually free from seven o'clock.'

There was no lightning smile, he was simply stating facts.

'Bring in the mail as soon as you're ready.'

The 'phone rang beside her and she answered it in her usual business-like manner wishing just for five minutes it would be quiet. Mark Findlay seemed to have twice as many 'phone calls as his sister and each one had to be handled with care. After the blast he had given her over his own 'phone call, she could only hope that he appreciated her efforts.

'Anna, my darling, my beautiful one, I've been thinking of you. You've given me hope.'

'Maurice! I'm sorry, I can't talk to you now,' she spoke firmly.

'Anna, wait! I must see you. When do you get some time off! I must talk to you.'

'I don't think that's wise, Maurice. Goodbye.'

She heard a faint sound and her eyes widened as Mark appeared in the doorway. Clearly, the open door allowed him to check her conversations.

She replaced the receiver and he swung back to his desk with a brief query about a price list. She fetched it, then sat down tapping out the letter, her fingers flying. He had told her not to get involved with Maurice Caswell. She had no intention of doing so, but Mark had no right to tell her whom she could or could not meet. In office time his words might have some justification but outside the office she was able to make her own decisions! Anna pulled out the letter and she took it into Mark for his signature. He read it through and frowned.

'You'll have to do it again. This top figure's wrong. Check, don't guess.'

Wordlessly she took the paper back and returned to her desk. She checked her notes then saw that she had been at fault. It didn't help. She should have picked it up herself but she had been so annoyed over Mark supervising her call. The mistake infuriated her. Mark stood beside her as she finished and knowing that he was reading the work as her fingers flew did not help. He signed it, then handed it back to her.

'Stop for a moment and take a short letter, please.'

Obediently Anna picked up her shorthand pen, aware of his proximity. She summoned up her courage to face him, trying to match his apparent indifference.

He turned away and began dictating. 'Thank you for following my instructions with regard to Maurice Caswell. The situation is more complex than you would realise. Stop. New para. I regret my actions last evening; as you said, business and pleasure can be a dangerous combination. Sign it, with apologies, from Mark Findlay and send it to Anna Heathley.'

His grin broke as she realised the content of the letter and her fingers stopped. Anna found her own smile meeting his instinctively.

'Take an hour off, Anna. We'll both be better for it. I'm off to get in a round of golf. I'll switch on my telepager. If you need me urgently, give me a signal and I'll return. Don't do it unless you have to, it's a trifle off-putting to one's putting to have it bleep!'

It was almost a joke thought Anna, but she was too conscious of him to do more than nod.

'Here's the number. You dial it on the 'phone and then hang up. I will hear the signal and return to the office. You can use that to call me when I'm in the Christchurch area and I'll simply stop at the first 'phone and ring you. Clear?'

'Yes.'

He went off and a moment later she heard a lively whistling as he crossed the lawn in front of the house. Anna watched as John joined him, two golf-trolleys mute evidence that he had planned the diversion. It reminded her that she had to take the letter along to Sally and she put the 'phones on to record and walked to the kitchen.

'Anna, a cup of tea?'

'I'd love one. I'm feeling slightly frayed.'

She gave Sally the letter as the kettle boiled.

'Now, Anna, just sit and put your feet up. Miss Penelope always used to relax when Mark and John went golfing together. Both of them enjoy it tremendously. You've at least two hours before he returns and sometimes it's longer. How was the evening?'

'It wasn't an unmitigated success, shall we say. The hotel was magnificent, and the food was superb. It was . . .' she hesitated, 'interesting. I ran into an old friend, Maurice Caswell, who happened to have married a friend of Mark's.'

'I can imagine,' put in Sally. 'Clare was one of Mark's first girl friends.'

Sally put the cup down slowly and Anna knew that she was studying her words. 'We were glad Clare married someone else.' As though she had said too much she picked up her bag. 'Goodness, look at the time, I must rush.'

Anna drank her tea alone, but her thoughts were whirling. Was the beautiful Clare, the reason why Mark was still a bachelor?

CHAPTER FIVE

ANNA rinsed out her teacup and returned to the office. With luck she could clear the mail while Mark was away.

Some were complex and after her blunder that morning she checked and rechecked, slowing her normal, automatic process. As twelve o'clock approached she took it into his office then straightened the mess she had made of the files that morning.

Finished she looked at the garden and decided to walk along the pleasant grounds for a few minutes. She opened the door and moved to the edge of the trees, yet within hearing distance of the 'phones. Part of the golf course was directly behind the trees and some distance away she could see Mark swing a club. The small, white ball sailed obediently towards the patch of green, gingham checked lawn, only a few feet away from where she stood.

A moment later John repeated the manoeuvre, his ball landing close to the flag. Anna stepped back hurriedly as the men sauntered towards the green. The trees screened her as she continued to watch and she smiled, noting how relaxed and almost boyish Mark looked in comparison with the man who had been so abrupt with her earlier in the office.

'I could have sworn I'd got onto the green,' Mark commented. 'Must have overshot though and rolled into the dip. Take yours, John. See if you can get a birdie.'

He stood silently, then smiled as John rolled his ball over to the flag.

'You beat me. Well done! For punishment you can look for my ball while I check over here.'

Anna stood uncertain, trapped between the two searching figures. Reluctantly she stepped out.

'If you're looking for the ball it went into the hole.'

There was an incredulous gasp from the two men. Anna moved a little hesitantly. Both men turned and checked the hole. John's ball was claimed and Mark dug the second ball out, holding it aloft, with a shout. His grin was like sunshine after rain.

'You little beauty!'

He twirled her, waltzing round the green to John's clapping. Anna was surprised. He seemed so overjoyed about finding it that she looked at him puzzled. He hadn't seemed like a man who worried about losing a ball.

He stopped to explain. 'It's a hole in one, Anna.'

'That's good, isn't it?'

They both laughed. Mark's arm had been lightly around her shoulders and his touch sent strange shivers running through her.

'You've brought me luck, Anna. It's the sort of shot golfers dream about. I did one when I was a kid, a sheer fluke. John's done three in a lifetime of golf.' He grinned at her, all antagonism vanished.

'Anna, I'll have to teach you to play. Tomorrow what appointments have I booked in?'

'You're due in town at one-thirty and again at two.'

'Right. At ten o'clock I'll give you your first lesson.'

He glanced at his watch.

'We'll just get cleaned up and be in to lunch. I suppose that's why you came out. Did Sally ask you to put the meal on? Five minutes all right with you, John?'

Anna turned away. She sped back to the kitchen wondering how she was going to produce a meal in that time in a strange kitchen. She need not have worried. Sally had arranged a smorgasbord in the dining room and it was only a matter of removing the cover and plugging in the kettle. It had just boiled when the pair returned, still elated by the feat.

The meal was fun, clearly the joy of the occasion had made Mark forget his secretary's deficiencies. The afternoon work was fascinating, Mark explaining some of the complex regulations in such a way that they seemed a different set of documents from the volumes of verbiage she had tried to study before.

She recalled Catherine Lester's comment that with Mark she would learn a great deal and knew that it was true. His eyes rewarded her when she picked up a detail and when the computers tapped out a message shortly before five he asked her to make a decision on it and prepare her notes.

It was like sitting an exam, she thought ruefully, but the knowledge that Mark was preparing himself equally, challenged her. When she was satisfied she took it into him and waited anxiously for his verdict.

'You've done well. Your premise here is wrong, but as we haven't covered that I can't blame you. You're a promising student.'

He smiled at her and Anna felt as if she had been given a bonus. She was almost sorry when it was time for her to leave the office.

The swimming pool was tempting and when she heard Mark drive away, she made the most of his absence. In the evening, she joined John and Sally watching television and when she found the clock turning to ten she went to bed, well pleased with her day. The thought of Mark teaching her to play golf sent her to sleep with a smile.

With their new rapport, work on the mail in the morning was swift and even some complex, detailed analysis which Mark asked her to prepare, went together smoothly.

When John joined them at ten o'clock with some clubs for her she submitted patiently as the two men adjudged the height of the clubs and their weight. It was a foreign language as far as she was concerned but she swung the club in the seriousness that the pair demanded. She sighed with relief when John disappeared with the clubs and returned with a trolley and a bag containing a gleaming highly polished set.

'You should find those just right, Anna,' Mark commented. 'John's very good at judging clubs for a person. Switch the 'phones and let's go.'

She pushed the trundler noting the different shapes and sizes of the clubs.

Mark pointed to the wooden-headed clubs, with their carved edges. 'Those are called woods, you use them for long driving shots usually.'

'Try and hit the ball on that side.' He grinned

and she could tell it would be impossible to do so anywhere else. She risked a smile.

'I'll probably lose the ball,' she warned.

'I doubt it. You probably won't even hit it. I asked John to turn the sprinklers off on one and two. We'll start on those holes and you can see how you feel after that.'

'Is John not coming with us?' she queried, as the older man sauntered off in the direction of a shed.

'No, he's got his work to do,' Mark replied. 'It's a full time occupation keeping the ground in order and he has very little assistance. Besides, I couldn't bear to see his face when you dig up half his precious fairway.'

'Thanks very much!' she answered. 'You do give a girl confidence, don't you?'

She was no longer sure that she wanted to learn. And, she thought crossly, he hadn't even asked her, just told her and expected her to be delighted.

'Right, this small rise here with the markers is where you stand to drive the ball down the strip of grass. It's called teeing off. You aim for the hole at the base of the flag. It's two hundred and ten metres, just a nice distance to start you off.'

He plucked a small orange pin from his pocket and set it in the ground. 'This is the tee, you use it only at the start of each hole.'

He put a ball on top and Anna stood eyeing it nervously. It wasn't a very big ball, she decided, and the length of the clubs was disconcerting. She had seen the occasional game on television and the easy, apparently relaxed stance of the

players, but she felt like a rigid, iron stake, stiff
and unyielding.

'Now, take this wood and hold it like this.'
Mark demonstrated and she tried to grip it in the
approved manner.

'No! Like this.' He took her hand and held it
with his own. Anna was very aware of his body
and the faint tang of crisp aftershave he wore.
Her fingers felt like limp pieces of straw, which
she tried to tighten as he suggested.

'That's better. Now take a couple of practice
swings.'

Trying to keep her fingers in the right position,
she lifted the club back and then swung it down
towards the ground. Shaking his head regretfully,
Mark came up to her.

'Like this; keep your head down and swing
right through your whole body.'

He took her arms and with his own encompassing
her, held them in position. She was far too aware of
the warmth of his body and the steady thump of his
heart. It was not helpful to know that her own was
doing a copy of a sound track for an international
ping-pong competition. Amazingly the 'thwack' of
the club connecting with the ball sounded. Anna
was never certain how she had managed to hit the
ball.

'There you are, just as easy as that, now here's
another. Do exactly the same.'

She eyed the little ball and tried to make up
her mind whether she could by some miracle hit
it again. Mark stood at the side and the
knowledge that he was watching every move,
made her concentrate. She held her arms in the
correct position, the ball in line with the instep

of her left heel and swung.

It sailed away and she stared after it in delighted disbelief.

'Pretty good, next time try not to drop the club.'

The dry comment brought her back to earth.

'You're not playing baseball.'

He placed another ball on the tee. Sometimes she hit the ball, at other times she hit the ground in front of her with a bone shuddering jar and several times the earth rose spectacularly, instead of the ball. Mark picked up the divots of earth and grass and carefully placed them back on the ground.

'We'll start playing. You count each stroke. As we go down you can pick up those other balls.'

'Yes, sir,' she muttered.

It was all very well for him to look pityingly at her play, he had been playing all his life; he'd probably been born with a club in his hand with his attitude to women, she thought savagely. There was a great deal of the caveman about him.

She gritted her teeth and forgot everything she had practised so carefully, just swiping instinctively at the ball. It rode high in the air and she watched as it sailed halfway towards the target.

'Now that was good,' he said, 'why couldn't you have done that before?'

She was so annoyed that she stormed up to the ball and slammed it again, pretending to herself that she was aiming at the curl that hung boyishly down. The ball sailed with the greatest of ease and she decided that perhaps after all she might make the grade as a golfer, if only by thinking of Mark Findlay all the time. Rapidly she collected the other balls, Mark putting them into the bag as he pulled the trolley.

'Now, you'll have to forget what I told you a moment ago about your feet position, with the iron you stand differently.'

Again his arms went round her and she found herself very conscious of his lean, hard strength as he positioned her arms and demonstrated the swing. His mouth was on a level with her eyes and the shape of his lips was curving and well cut. It was decidedly off putting, she thought, as his eyes met hers. Hastily she looked at the small, white ball. He released her and she tried to concentrate but it was hopeless.

The ball dribbled along the ground and she replaced it and tried again. Mark's smothered laughter suddenly gave her muscles their power and she swung, hitting the ball with all the force she could muster. It rose beautifully, sailing above the flag and on to another fairway.

'It's supposed to go in this hole first, before you move on to that one,' he commented drily. 'Leave it there and take another ball.'

Ignominiously she reached for another and tried again and by sheer good fortune it bounced and skidded its way towards the chequered patch.

'You're just on the green by a blade of grass! Use the flat one, the putter, to hit it towards the hole. I'll hold the flag for you.'

It took her ten attempts to get it into the hole, by which time she was feeling that golf and she were to be sworn enemies.

'I've never seen anyone so bad,' Mark commented, with a rueful shake of his head. 'There's a putting green just outside the office, you might have noticed. If you get a bit of spare time I suggest you try a little practice. Let's get on to the next hole.'

He led the way and she followed meekly. It could hardly be worse, she consoled herself. It was! And the third was just the same. Her shoulders ached, her waist and hips hurt, her fingers resigned themselves as she jarred against the ground for the dozenth time. Each time Mark winced for her and she looked at him pleadingly.

'This is a game? Are you sure?'

'Yes, it's great! Look, it's so easy.' He took the club from her weary arms and swung it effortlessly, the ball landing on the green. 'See?'

His telepager suddenly bleeped and he glanced at his watch.

'May as well go in, you won't be able to work if you don't stop now.'

He said it with a cheeky grin to remove the sting but the fact remained it was the truth, she thought tiredly.

He pushed the trundler ahead of her and as she staggered across the lawn he ran to the kitchen to check the message with Sally. After a quick shower she felt revitalised and made her way to the kitchen. Sally and John were there and she gave them an account which sent them into gales of laughter.

'Oddly enough Anna could make a good golfer, she did three decent shots which were amazingly good,' Mark commented as he entered the room.

'I think I'll stick to swimming,' she muttered.

Three pairs of eyes stared at her in astonishment, as though her words had been heresy. Golf

was a game to which she was not suited. At least
not when Mark Findlay was the coach and his
touch wrecked her self control!

It was almost a relief to return to the office.
Mark was just collating a few notes for his
appointments in Christchurch when the 'phone
rang again. He waited beside her, expecting the
call to be for him and he smiled as she answered.
She felt her heart pound, softening her voice so
that her answer was slightly breathless. The
responding sound crashed her to the earth.

'Anna, darling. Can you talk? I'm desperate to
see you.'

Mark was only a foot away from her and he
reached over for the 'phone, taking it from her.
His lips formed a straight line as he listened
momentarily and heard Maurice's words.

'Anna can't talk to you now and she won't in
future. Clear?' Mark said crisply. He put
down the receiver, cutting off the deluge of
words.

'I'm entitled to meet friends after work if I
wish,' said Anna, her own temper flaring at his
highhanded action.

'*Not* Maurice Caswell!'

His eyes were like glittering glacial ice. He
picked up his case. Deliberately he went to the
books they had studied the afternoon before.

'When you've finished the work I've left you,
copy out the next two chapters and study them.
I'll go over it when I return.'

He strode out of the doorway and Anna glared
after him. To crash back to the cold war
atmosphere was disheartening. The pile in front
of her would keep her glued to her chair; since

lunch they had more than made up for the loss of the earlier time.

It was four-fifteen when she tiredly eased her shoulders and neck and looked rebelliously at the volumes he had told her to copy. Her glance went to the photocopier and she grinned, thinking that he had not used the word 'type'. She could copy out the pages and still have time for a swim before Mark Findlay returned!

A minute later she left the photostated copies on top of his desk, slammed the 'phones to the recorder and ran along the hall to her room. It took her only a brief time to change and slip out to the gently lapping pool. The temperature of the water was cool on her skin and she shivered momentarily as she adjusted. It was lovely and relaxing, lying blissfully in the water, just closing her eyes and letting the water play 'touch me, touch me not', with her toes. She smiled impishly at the thought of the photostated copies and rolled over in the water then began paddling about, doing her own lazy version of a side stroke, just enough to send the water glissading over her shoulder. Time became just a pattern of the odd, fluffy clouds moving against the sky until the thought of a certain man's return drove her to the edge.

She need not have worried. It was after midnight when she heard the car return to the house and she wondered why she should have remained sleepless, the memory of a freezing glance and glittering anger disturbing her.

There was no friendly greeting in the morning. Instead the photocopied sheets were on her desk. The atmosphere in the office was like a wind direct from Antartica. It was cold and hard and he saw that her every moment was occupied.

Over the following few days she warily began to build up a respect for his sheer ability and hard work. Grudgingly, she was forced into conceding the man deserved his success, he was well informed enough to have no inhibitions about checking when he did enter a field outside his expertise. Not afraid to make decisions, he studied the options and reports and then acted. He seemed to be held in great affection by his friends and the agents held him in considerable respect.

But, thought Anna, the line was drawn at his acting secretary. He gave her the work and left her to it. She might have had the feelings of the computer sitting in the office, as far as he was concerned. Despite his coldness, she knew she was learning. Her knowledge was increasing all the time and she could see more clearly than before the complex network he controlled.

Not once did he offer to help her as she struggled to understand and she could have wept in frustration when she remembered the brilliance of the earlier lessons.

Yet she had to admit that never had she worked in such wonderful surroundings and Sally and John were kind and anxious to help. Although she never said a word, she knew they guessed at the boss's attitude to her as she was sent to have her lunch an hour earlier, which meant she dined in splendid isolation. Breakfast, Sally and John had together, in their flat and by the time she appeared, Mark had started his office routine. He was seldom in the house in the

evening and she guessed that he was seeing Clare
Caswell.

She took the last letter out of the typewriter as
Mark entered her office.

'After you've finished that you may take the
afternoon off. Can you be here from eight till
eleven tonight?'

'Yes.'

'I'll see you then.'

She gathered the papers together and gave
them to him. He nodded but was otherwise non-
committal. Wearily she made her way to her
room and changed from her business suit to a
sundress. Paddling barefoot across the lawn to
the kitchen, she smiled at Sally who held aloft a
teapot.

'I'd love a cup.'

'First time I've seen you looking relaxed for a
few days,' Sally commented. 'Mark letting you
off the chain for an afternoon?'

'You put it correctly,' smiled Anna. 'I'm not
sure how Miss Penelope stands the pace.'

'She seems to thrive on it,' put in John,
walking in at that moment. 'Did I hear the kettle
boil?'

'Smells a teapot, does John Carter!' laughed
Sally. She turned to her husband. 'Anna has the
afternoon off. What about giving her a few
pointers on golf, dear?'

'Sure, no trouble at all. We'll go out straight
after this drink.'

His wife smiled so approvingly that Anna
didn't have the heart to say that the last thing she
felt like doing was striving to hit a small, white
ball. If it was decorated with a picture of the

managing director of a certain import-export business, she might have more success.

'Will the boss be joining us?' John looked at her enquiringly.

She could only hope not.

'I don't know. If he wants to play, you go with him. I can just practise on my own.'

'Right, let's get started.'

John's enthusiasm for his task made her shake her head warningly. 'I can't seem to hit the ball very easily.'

'That's only the first step. I'm sure you'll make a golfer.'

His confidence was endearing and after the harsh attitude of their boss, it was a welcome contrast. She decided to forget Mark. It was her time off, she needn't think about him!

Oddly enough she began to relax and enjoy herself. Without Mark standing beside her, telling her to move her arm up or down or straighten it, she relaxed and to her delight actually managed to hit the ball every time.

'There you are! Nothing to it!' John commended her. 'You just needed a little confidence.'

With John it didn't matter if she connected the club with the ball. She felt unbelievable delight as the ball sailed towards the distant green.

'A good one!'

John took out his own ball and club. 'Might as well play if you're going to hit great shots like that!'

An hour later they made their way back to the green by the house.

'You've probably done enough now. You did very well.'

Anna smiled. 'Thanks, John. You know, I think I'm beginning to see why people like golf.'

'I'll take you out tomorrow if the boss let's you out of his sight long enough.'

She managed a weak grin. Instinctively she looked towards the house and saw Mark walking towards the swimming pool, his arm around the shoulders of a dark-haired, curvaceous woman. Anna felt anger dart through her. It was too much. He had the temerity to tell her who not to see, yet he had the gall to take out the man's wife!

'I've got to collect a few things from town. I'll only be there an hour, if you want a ride.' John looked at her.

Anna's eyes went to the couple sitting beside the pool. It wouldn't be much fun sitting in her suite with that picture engraved on her mind.

'Thanks, I'll get changed. Five minutes?'

'I'll give you ten.'

They went up to the back entrance of the homestead and avoided by unspoken consent the pair at the pool. Ten minutes later Anna looked at the road as John handled the wheel with the experience of years.

The paddocks formed a green and gold crossword puzzle, the fences and hedges the connecting lines and the occasional houses the blanks. But she had few clues on how to handle the enigma at the centre, Mark Findlay.

John dropped her off in the Square and for an hour she sauntered around the immediate area, 'doing' the square in the manner of a tourist, inspecting the towering Gothic church in grey stone and the shopping mall and arcades in the adjacent area. The fashion shops delighted her, there seemed to be so many boutiques and salons specialising in frothy, frivolous clothes. She decided that the next time she had time to herself, she would explore them further, but as her hour was up she went back towards the meeting place.

'John, I found some wonderful shops,' she greeted him. 'I must get some time off organised and have a look around. Otherwise I'll be heading back to Wellington next week and I'll not have seen a thing.'

'Next week? I thought you'd be here till Miss Penelope returns,' John said innocently. 'That's what Mark said, at any rate.'

'Oh no, I'm only here for two weeks.' She frowned a little. Catherine had been in frequent communication over a complex deal, but Anna hadn't asked if her replacement was organised.

'The boss isn't often wrong,' said John, as he changed gear for a green traffic light.

The car powered away and Anna wasn't certain if the sudden sickening thrust of her body was the response to the swift movement of the car or the news that she might be left with Mark Findlay. She shivered, knowing that if Mark Findlay had decided on something, it was almost as good as done. All she could hope was that John had misinterpreted his words.

'He thinks you're a first class secretary, told me so the second day. Mind you, he wouldn't have had you around this long if you weren't doing the job.'

It was nice to get a compliment, even if it was secondhand. Then she frowned, remembering that at that time their relationship was not soured by Maurice Caswell. Seeing she had offended him, she could be sent home next week after all. She was surprised when she felt chagrin at the prospect. A minute earlier she had been dreading the thought of staying on for another four weeks, yet at the prospect of a swift departure, she felt disturbingly disappointed.

The conundrum bothered her. Mark Findlay was just a man, used to beautiful women falling at his feet. She certainly wasn't going to join their ranks. An irritating niggle informed her tartly that since her insult he had been far from attempting to charm her!

At eight o'clock she went along to the office and looked around. For once there was no sign of Mark Findlay. Her desk had several notes ready for her and she studied them and began work.

Automatically she checked the 'phone and then settled to continue work. Just as she was deep in the third one the telephone rang and she answered it, thinking it could well be Mark telling her he was delayed.

'Anna, it's Maurice. Don't tell me you're working now, it's eight-thirty!'

'Very well, Maurice, I won't tell you, but as the only time I answer this 'phone is when I'm working, I'll let you draw your own conclusion,' she answered a little warily, hoping Mark would not enter while she was talking.

'Anna, darling, I must see you! Tomorrow evening meet me at the turn-off. I won't embarrass you by picking you up at the house. I need to talk to you. I'll be there at seven-thirty and I'll wait until eight. Please, Anna.'

'Maurice, four years ago you made a choice. I

don't see how discussing the present situation will help.'

She had a mental picture of Mark Findlay walking across to the swimming pool, his arm around Clare Caswell's shoulders. A rush of mixed emotions weakened her resolve.

'Please, Anna.'

'Maurice, I have the strangest feeling I'll regret it, but I will meet you if the boss doesn't need me. I'm sorry I can't be more definite than that.'

'That's my wonderful Anna.'

She put down the 'phone and stared at it for a moment, full of misgivings. Maurice Caswell meant nothing to her, but meeting him was going directly against the wishes of Mark Findlay. Crossly she reminded herself that it was all his fault! If he hadn't been so arrogant about whom she met she could have talked at length on the phone and dealt with the situation at a distance. Mark Findlay had no right to organise her private life!

CHAPTER SIX

A moment later Anna heard Mark whistling as he approached the office. It was just as well he hadn't overheard her conversation with Maurice. She checked the figures he had given her and settled to type in the next series into the computer. By the time he arrived five minutes later, she was reading the printout copy.

'Ring Catherine for me. Any developments?'

She handed the computer sheets to him and he ran his hand quickly down the column of figures. While he was looking she dialled his sister's number.

'Catherine Lester speaking.'

'Good evening. It's Anna here.'

'Anna, my dear, how are you enjoying Orakau. I hear you are turning into a golfer.'

'A gopher, more likely! I tend to show my farming background and till the soil.' She became aware of Mark standing beside her and her laughter died. 'Catherine, Mark wishes to speak to you, but before he does, can I ask you about my relief?'

'My dear, of course. My new girl isn't a patch on you. Still, she is very obliging and willing to learn.'

'Do you think she could take over from me next week?'

She saw Mark looking at her, one eyebrow raised and he held out his hand for the receiver. Weakly she handed it over.

'Catherine? What's this nonsense?' He listened momentarily. 'No, I don't. I'm not training someone else. Anna stays here till Miss Penelope returns. Clear?'

His eyes smouldered as he looked at Anna sitting miserably by the desk.

'I don't care if Anna has a face as long as a cello, so long as she does the work I require.' His voice was sharp. 'And at the moment it's threatening to turn into a double bass.' He swung round on the desk as though the sight of her was enough to put anyone into the miseries.

'Catherine, I've just got the results we wanted. It looks feasible. Security wise it could be tricky, but so long as only the three of us know we needn't work out a computer code. If we do decide to go ahead we'll do one then.'

Anna was interested in his conversation despite her annoyance. Only Mark Findlay could be so dictatorial. It was all right for his sister to train a relief but he wasn't going to be upset! Mutinously she glared at his broad back. She pulled a face and he swung back to meet it and he grinned unexpectedly and pulled a worse one back.

'No, of course Anna won't object. Sleep well, little sis.'

He smiled and Anna felt her heart pound at the sweetness of his face. It was a totally different look and it lightened his hard features. Anna looked at the papers in front of her. When she looked at her boss he met her look blandly.

'So, you want to go home?' A boyfriend who can't exist without you? Tough! Tell him he can stay here for a weekend if you like. There's plenty of room.'

He sauntered into his office and Anna felt her temper soar.

'Does that apply to Maurice Caswell?' she asked.

'You know full well it doesn't!'

Anna could have bitten her tongue, on hearing the frost back in his voice. She glared at the papers wondering why it was that Mark Findlay made her strike sparks so readily.

'Anna, I want to dictate some points which you can check on for me.'

It was back to work and she sighed as she picked up her notepad. Two hours later she put through another international call and her eyes went to the figures the deal promised. It seemed as if Mark Findlay was well on his way to pulling off another coup in the business world. Knowing their importance she checked them again and satisfied with the result she took them into Mark. He was just finishing the call and he dictated a series of quick reminders, then studied the notes.

'Quite satisfactory, Anna.' He glanced at her and a slight frown wrinkled his brow.

'You look tired. Go to bed. Start at eleven in the morning. John said you wanted to have some time to explore the shops. There's late night shopping till nine tomorrow so you can take from three o'clock off.'

'Thank-you. Will you need me tomorrow night?' She held her breath, thinking of her meeting with Maurice.

'No, I'm going out. I won't be able to get this affair in action till early next week.'

'Will I lock the papers in the safe?'

'No, I'll stay on a bit longer.' He smiled suddenly and it was as if the sun shone on a cold day. 'I'm barely getting started.'

She said goodnight and went slowly to her own room. She felt pleased and she knew that the satisfaction came not from her work but from the last smiling glance Mark had given her. Evidently he had concluded that she had heeded his request not to see Maurice. After the misery of the past few days when he had treated her like an automaton, the breakthrough was welcome.

To her relief work sped the next day. The difference in the atmosphere was marked. As she unplugged her typewriter at three o'clock she felt a sense of holiday, only vaguely troubled by her proposed meeting with Maurice.

'If you're intending to be back before seven you can take my car. Otherwise John or Sally could take you in and pick you up later.'

'I'll be back before seven,' she answered a little guiltily. She wondered if he had offered the limousine just to check up on her. I'm getting to be as suspicious as Mark Findlay, she told herself, as she slipped behind the wheel.

It was a pleasure driving the car. She smiled as it purred along, heading townwards. For a few moments she wondered about parking, then remembered the office parking spot always held for Mark's car.

The parking problem solved she began meandering along the banks of the River Avon. She was amused by the antics of a mother duck and her brood, the ducklings fluffy, little brown and yellow specks paddling in a trail behind the mother. When they began splitting up the mother would nudge one, and then another back to order, only to find the first had sailed away.

'You need Mark Findlay to bring a bit of discipline into your brood,' she said softly to the harried mother duck.

The duck quacked her response with a tone of such agreement that Anna laughed.

She crossed the Bridge of Remembrance to the Mall area she had found before and sauntered slowly among the shops. The knowledge that she had plenty of time made her view the world with rose tinted spectacles.

Her eyes went to a dress on display and she went closer to inspect it. Made of a soft, hand dyed silk in muted pinks, it hung in gathers from a straight yoke. It was just a sun dress style, but beside it lay a matching stole-like scarf which she realised could be worn as a belt or a novel head scarf or shoulder wrap. Tempted, she asked to try it on and a moment later stood viewing herself in the mirror.

'Lovely,' the shop girl's comment made her nod her head.

'Yes, it is.'

'Our designer is very intrigued with the colouring of the silks and she has made some really beautiful garments. But I must say that on you the dress looks superb. Your colouring is shown to perfection with the tonings of pink.'

She slipped the belt into place then allowed the attendant to tie a small knot. Then she tried it around her head and tucked it into place. The girl fetched a pin and they both experimented to get the best effect. After that she wound it around her neck.

'Dazzling!'

The shop girl was right, thought Anna. The dress had a deceptive air. It seemed very mild and gentle until it was on then it looked almost naughty in its sexiness with the scarf trailing from one shoulder.

'Your boyfriend's going to love you in it,' said the girl. 'Shall I wrap it for you?'

'Yes please,' said Anna, glancing at the price tag and shuddering mentally. She had guessed it would be expensive and she was right. But she could justify it on the reasoning that she had to have some more outfits to wear.

She had packed for two weeks, not six. A small voice whispered that she had bought it because she wanted Mark to notice her wearing it, but she ignored it. To Mark it wouldn't matter if she wore the traditional potato sack, so long as she completed the work he required. She grinned as she remembered that the humble potato sack had turned into plastic bags.

The dress bag was light and she carried it easily as she wandered around. It was relaxing just meandering through the shops, seeing the varied range of goods and inspecting the novelties. A band was giving an evening concert and she sat with some of the other shoppers listening to the music with enjoyment. It seemed amazing but she disregarded time so completely that it was a shock to realise that she should return if she was to have the limousine back by seven o'clock.

Mark was dressed to go out and his eyes danced when they saw the parcel.

'Ah! Making a retailer happy? You look pleased with yourself.'

'I am. It's really the prettiest dress, Mark.' Enthusiasm made her eyes light. 'I can justify it, I needed more clothes if I'm going to stay down here. I only packed for two weeks.'

'Sounds as though I should pay for it.' Again the lightning grin flashed. 'Leave the docket on my desk and I'll reimburse you for it. I'm glad you had a good day.'

He strode off, whistling as he went towards the car.

Anna went to her room. It was generous of Mark to offer to pay for the frock, but she wasn't going to take him up on it. Carefully she hung the dress up then changed into jeans and a blouse. If she was going to meet Maurice she was going to make it clear that she was not trying to interest him. She would give him ten minutes and try to convince him that she didn't wish to see him again, and that his marriage would be more likely to work if he spent more attention on his wife.

Her frown deepened as she slipped out of the house. She didn't like subterfuge and she wished she'd never agreed to the meeting. For four years she had thought herself in love with Maurice and he hadn't so much as bothered to give her a 'phone call. Now she had crossed his path, he was urgently wanting to meet her. Sadly her lips twisted. She had been so much in love with Maurice, his good looks and his charm, she had overlooked his roving eyes and been happy 'to accept his 'business' trips to Christchurch. The announcement of his engagement had shocked her completely. She had been so naïve, she thought bitterly, so innocently trusting of Maurice.

She wondered how long she would have gone on using the safety screen of Maurice to protect her from other advances. It had become so automatic to give any man the brush off, letting them know loud and clear that she had her own life and she wasn't risking it in anyone's hands but her own.

Maurice's low slung car was a powerful, exotic model and she smiled. Maurice had got exactly what he wanted.

'Anna, darling.'

Maurice stepped out as she approached. She took his hands rather than have him kiss her as he so clearly intended.

'Maurice, this is ridiculous,' Anna began firmly.

'I agree, darling, but it's what you wanted. I've missed you. I hadn't realised until I saw you the other night. You're so beautiful Anna, so much my lovely Anna.' His hand went to hold her but she slipped away.

'Please, Maurice, I . . .'

'Darling, you don't have to say a word. I'll take care of everything. I'll take you to this beautiful spot I know and there we can really get to know each other again. Get in the car, my darling.'

'Maurice, I . . .'

'Hush, no talking now.'

He cut off her attempt at speech and glanced worriedly around as though he expected Mark's heavy hand to pounce on him at any moment.

'Look, Maurice, I'm not going anywhere.'

'Please darling, we can't talk here.'

The thought of Mark going past made her reluctantly take her seat. Maurice started the car immediately. He was silent for a moment as he concentrated on driving. Anna glanced at the mileage readout and didn't like the way the numbers were flashing past.

'Maurice, can we stop and talk? I've no desire to go driving round the countryside with you.'

He pulled up down a side road near a little settlement where trees formed a thick screen, sheltering the car from the road.

He smiled at her and his fingers went to brush her lips. Suddenly she had no doubts as to his intentions.

'Maurice, I don't feel in the least attracted to you. There's no point in sitting inside this greenhouse making polite conversation.'

'Darling Anna.'

'It's darling Clare, remember? When I agreed to this meeting I thought I might be able to talk to you, but that's not what you want.'

'But I love you, you love me,' he expostulated. Clearly the thought of a repulse hadn't entered his mind. 'I thought we could be together darling. I know you expected us to marry, Anna, but we had so little money. I hoped that I would forget you but I never did, darling.'

He looked at her earnestly and Anna remembered the look with a grin for her own former naïvety. Once that look would have made her heart flip. If it failed he always looked hurt and sorrowful. When his lower lip pouted it almost made her laugh and she wondered how she could not have seen through his predictable behaviour years before.

'Anna, when we danced together the other night I knew we belonged together.' He realised that she was smiling at him, and his expression sharpened.

'You're such a beautiful creature, you drive men crazy with that cool, touch me not air. I want you, my darling, as much as you want me.'

Anna attempted a lighthearted reply.

'Great! I don't want you at all so nobody's hurt!'

'You don't want me?' He seemed genuinely surprised, 'then you must be in love. I know, you're in love with Mark Findlay!'

'Me! In love with Mark? Nonsense!'

'It's true, that's why you don't want me.'

He nodded as though he could accept defeat at the hands of another man, but not from her.

'Mark's got you exactly where he wants you, hasn't he? At his beck and call all day and all night.'

'You'd better take me back right now,' Anna said quietly. 'I don't think your words are sensible of my dignity or Mark's.'

Maurice started the car. They drove back to the turn-off in icy silence.

'You can take me to the door,' Anna commented as he slowed down his approach.

'Not likely! Get an earful from your boss as well as from you? Lady Anna, you can walk back.'

He pulled up and Anna climbed out gladly.

Only then did Maurice's face clear.

'I suppose I should have expected you to be angry with me. I'm sorry, Anna. You really did want to help, didn't you? Goodbye.'

The car seemed to spit gravel at her angrily as he powered away. Slowly she walked towards the house nestled comfortably among the trees. It looked peaceful, she thought tiredly. The scene with Maurice had drained her. He was so wrong! She in love with Mark Findlay? It was a joke! Except that she wasn't laughing.

A few days later Mark was working overtime as he made the last few checks on the big deal.

'Anna, I think we can say goodbye to the whole thing. Look at the share prices. Someone else has worked out the same deal.' He studied the figures thoughtfully. 'It's exactly the plan I was going to use. Wonder who it is?'

'Another investment company?'

'Possible. I guess we'll hear soon enough. Win some, lose some. I knew the risk in stalling action while I gathered funds.'

He was a remarkable man, she thought admiringly. He had worked really hard on the deal and had taken the blow manfully.

'Right, let's get on.'

The knowledge caused a shift in their plans for the funds available and the next few days were spent in further investigation and company reports. The old antagonism had gone completely.

Several times he went out of his way to explain why he made certain decisions. Each morning Anna looked forward to the day's activities, finding the work fascinating. The evenings she usually spent in the pool. Mark disappeared around teatime and she was never given any clue as to his whereabouts.

Anna tried telling herself it was no business of hers just where her boss was in his free time, but she found herself wondering and the sound of his jaunty, happy whistle haunted her.

In the office he was the perfect boss, she should be grateful for that. Yet that was the source of a vague irritation, the knowledge that to him she was merely a secretary there to take letters and do readouts, decode messages and very little else. At least she had plenty of time for golf and John had promised that he would take her for a proper round. She looked up as she heard laughter coming from the corridor.

'Well, if you won't take me I'll take your secretary, Mark.'

Clare Caswell entered the room. She looked devastatingly pretty.

'Hello, Anna. This boss of yours won't take me round for a few holes, so grab your clubs and come on.'

Mark entered behind the petite figure. He looked at Anna.

'Yes, Anna, you might as well. I'm wanting some peace and quiet for an hour and a half. Make sure you're back then.'

'But I'm hopeless,' she exclaimed hastily.

'Nonsense, off you go.'

Mark smiled and took her by the shoulder gently propelling her to the door. For his own reasons he wanted her out of it and entertaining his girlfriend. Sourly Anna stumped off to the games area where the clubs were kept. She joined Clare at the tee off for the first hole. Clare was already sending her ball driving expertly down the fairway.

Anna reluctantly pulled out her wood. She had to remember all the pointers which John had told her. Was it to keep the ball in line with the heel of the left foot? Or was that for the iron?

She looked hopefully towards the target. Under John's kindly eye the flag hadn't appeared so far away. Clare was waiting quietly. It made Anna tense, seeing the expression on Clare's face. She swung wildly and completely missed the ball. Clare's expression spoke volumes. Anna took her second shot more carefully and the ball struggled to skip and bounce forward.

'Not much better, really,' Clare commented.

'I am new to the game,' Anna said apologetically, as she followed the ball. 'If you'd prefer to play on your own, I'd be more than happy to walk round with you.'

'Most beginners need a little advice. Try again and concentrate.'

There was a hint of sarcasm which Anna could hardly ignore. She hit the ball and felt a disproportionate sense of relief when it rose magnificently. It was a good shot. Moments later Clare swung expertly, landing her ball very close to the green.

'That was a beauty,' Anna said generously.

'If a beginner had done it, yes, but it's only average for me.' Clare replaced her club.

The comment did not improve Anna's temper. When she reached her ball she hit it savagely and it powered over the other side of the green.

'You should have used an eight or a nine for that shot.'

Anna forebore to tell Clare that she had used the nine iron. She landed the ball on to the green, then fetched her putter. Clare placed her ball in the hole with two putts.

'I thought I may as well put mine in. You'll be all day,' Clare said.

Anna held her temper in check and wished Clare's statement was not so likely to be prophetic. She looked at the hole on the other side of the green. She remembered how Mark had shown her. Carefully she aimed and hit the ball. Incredibly it went in.

Clare looked at her. 'Lucky fluke?'

'Yes, it was.'

She pushed her trundler down towards the next hole. She had a sneaking suspicion Clare Caswell wanted her to look silly. She grinned. She knew her score would be enormous, with or without Clare!

Again Clare played a good shot and looking after it Anna sighed inwardly. There was no hope that her ball would go anywhere near the length, if she was lucky enough to strike it.

At least, Anna told herself humorously some holes later, she was getting five times as much exercise as Clare and she was seeing all parts of the course. By the time she reached the ninth hole, she had realised that quite apart from her own inadequacy, Clare had an uncanny knack of addressing some remark just as she started her shot. It succeeded every time in putting her off.

'You'll be due back in a short time. You may as well play the ninth hole, it brings you back towards the golf shed.'

Clare addressed Anna as though she was some sort of idiot.

'You're right. I believe it's your honour.' Anna indicated the tee off position. Clare took careful aim and swung. To Anna's secret delight she muffed it, missing it completely.

'Just a practice shot,' exclaimed Clare.

She hit the ball accurately down the fairway and Anna hid her grin. Every time she had done a similar shot, Clare had laughed unkindly. Anna decided that she didn't care if she muffed every one of the last shots. After playing with Clare she could play with anyone. She relaxed and sent her ball flying towards the green.

'Lucky!' assessed Clare.

Anna ignored her. Clare played her ball, then they walked together to Anna's ball. It lay white on the green of the fairway and a blade of grass rubbed against the side as though it was winking at her. The thought cheered Anna and she swung at it, quite prepared for Clare's cutting remark.

For once it didn't upset her, she knew she was doing it deliberately and shut out the words. The ball plopped down unbelievably on the green. There was a moment's silence from Clare as though she couldn't believe her eyes. Anna didn't blame her, after her previous game, the difference was startling.

Clare took her own ball and placed it carefully. She hit a fair shot but it still did not reach the green. Again she tried and her ball rolled straight to the pin. She smiled catlike.

'A satisfactory game. I won by so much it would be a bore to count the scores. Incidentally, it's not only golf I can beat you at. You'll be sorry you went out with my husband.'

The remark was so unexpected that Anna gasped. She stood by her ball, suddenly sick at heart.

'I did see Maurice briefly. I'm not in the least bit interested in him.'

'Don't bother to tell me lies. I've taken action to get rid of you. Mark thinks you're an excellent secretary. Just wait and see! It won't be long before he thinks differently!'

There was such venom in the woman's voice that Anna was troubled.

'Mark! Are you missing me?' Clare's abrupt change as she ran towards the shorts-clad figure who strode towards them was unbelievable. Anna looked in dismay as Clare tucked her arm proprietorially through his, smiling up at him.

'C'mon Anna. Let's see you get your first birdie.'

He smiled briefly at Clare and looked straight at Anna. She felt her heart flip as he met her gaze.

'Are you all right, Anna? You look very pale.'

'So she should!' Clare laughed. 'Look at her score.' She thrust the card under Mark's nose.

He glanced at it and then looked at Anna. 'Don't worry. Those last two shots were magnificent.'

'A tribute to my coaching.' Clare changed tactics quickly. 'Mark what would you advise Anna to use here?'

'I think Anna's quite capable of knowing which one to play,' he said quietly.

His eyes searched her face and his expression warmed her. Suddenly she felt better, pushing aside Clare's remarks. Mark was the boss and he was unlikely to dismiss her when he valued her secretarial skills.

She looked at the hole. It wasn't very far away.

She moved her arm back gently and stopped in mid-stroke, waiting for Clare's comment. A loud sneeze from Clare broke the silence. Ready for the interruption, Anna began again and sent the ball straight to the hole.

'You beauty!' Mark jubilantly hugged her but Anna was too aware of Clare's anger to relax.

'Thank you for the game.' Anna looked up at Mark. 'Will I go back to the office now?'

'No, go and have your lunch. I'll see you there in a few minutes.'

Clare didn't bother to say goodbye as Anna went towards the house. The knowledge that Mark was escorting Clare off the premises and not inviting her to stay made Anna feel quite surprisingly happy. She sat down to lunch and afterwards made for the shade of some overhanging trees. Mark joined her there. He looked puzzled and she remembered Clare's threat with some misgiving.

'Would you like a couple of days off? I've worked you rather hard, Anna.'

'You're paying. I don't feel particularly worn,' she grinned.

'You don't look it either.'

It was the first time he had come even remotely near paying her a compliment since the disastrous evening.

'I've got to take some papers over to the Lyttelton Harbour Board. You might like to come with me. We could visit Governor's Bay if you like.'

'That's over the Port Hills, isn't it?'

'Right. It is a very pretty spot. Trees, hills and sea,' he smiled.

'Playing hookey?' Anna asked cheekily. 'I'll be five minutes.'

Anna looked at her formal linen suit. It had been scarcely the gear to play golf in but at least the flared skirt had not hindered her too much but it certainly wasn't right for the beach. She ran to her room and flicked quickly through her clothes. Her eye fell on the soft pink silk and she hurriedly changed. A few minutes later she tied the scarf around a straw hat and slipped on the light sandals.

Mark's wolf whistle when he saw her made her heart stop beating for a moment. He tugged the end of the silk scarf playfully.

'Is this to tie some poor, helpless male up?' His eyes danced. 'You look very sexy, did you know that? I've got work to do.'

'Don't let me stop you,' she answered innocently and peeped up at him demurely from under her lashes.

His sapphire blue eyes teased and his mouth was a warm curve. 'Watch it, young woman.'

'Don't forget, you were the one to suggest taking time off.'

Mark followed the Ferry Road towards Summer and then turned towards the rock topped hills.

'There's the tunnel, Anna. It's a beauty, cuts out quite a steep haul.' Ahead was a long, glistening white, tiled expanse.

'How long is it? It seems to go on for ages,' she marvelled.

'It's two kilometres. The view's worth the wait,' said Mark as they approached the exit.

It was like arriving in another world. Ahead

the blue of the sea glittered, at the port. A
scattering of houses was sprinkled on the distant
hills, across the water.

'That's Diamond Harbour,' Mark informed
her. 'Some people travel across in the launch each
day to work. The terminal's just in front of us.
Around us is the port of Lyttelton, one day I'll
take you to see some of our containers being
loaded. I'll just drop these papers into the
Harbour Board office.'

Minutes later they swung away from the port
and followed the winding road towards the
country. The views of hills and sea kept Anna
spellbound as Mark guided the car. Houses clung
to the hillsides as they entered Corsair Bay and
then the road dipped to swing into another tiny
bay full of small boats.

A few minutes later it was left behind and the
road opened out. Trees marked Governor's Bay,
with the houses almost hidden by bush. The
occasional sheep moved on the hillsides above
them as Mark swung the car into a turnoff
marked by a shop and a hotel. The road
deteriorated as they drove past houses and a
school, towards the beach but Anna scarcely
noticed it, her eyes and ears delighting in the
sights and sounds. Mark pulled up with a smile
and his expression made her heart crash noisily
like the waves.

'The wind's up,' Mark commented.

He wandered over to the jetty reaching to the
sea. Anna looked around her at the orchestra of
green. It formed a harmony of colour, toning
from the blue of the gums against the sky, to the
lush willow green and the deep, dark green of the

bush areas, then led like a concerto theme back to the blue green of the sea.

The gentle wash of the waves slapping and swishing against the jetty and the line of rocks in front of her, made her turn to see Mark leaning against a post. He was looking out to sea and she wondered what he was thinking. His sunglasses hid his expression from her, but she guessed that even without them she would not have been able to see his thoughts. He was a lone wolf, who kept his own counsel.

She wondered why the thought should trouble her so much and she turned away following the line of the old road round the edge of the bay. It didn't matter to her what Mark thought or did. He was just the boss and she had no intention of getting involved, did she?

CHAPTER SEVEN

MARK came off the jetty and joined her, the sea breeze lifting the little curls on his forehead so that instinctively she wanted to brush them back. His blue eyes danced. Somehow he seemed just as at home in the rugged countryside as he did at 'Orakau'.

'This is magnificent,' she commented, trying to keep down the sudden elation she felt.

'Naturally.'

He smiled again and her breath suddenly disappeared. She gasped quickly and reminded herself that it was just another business trip. Mark would have taken Miss Penelope if she had been there.

'Oh!' the comment burst from her as she looked round delightedly a moment later.

In front of her steep cliffs of clay and volcanic rock formed a tiny inlet. White daisies climbed rebelliously up the cliffs, and wild sweet peas, their magenta flowers like miniature peacocks, flaunted their vivid colour. A couple of willows screened a fence and her eyes widened. She slowed as Mark pushed open a small gate.

'Where are you going?' she asked in surprise.

'Just in here,' he grinned and his teeth shone white. 'I assure you, it's perfectly all right.'

Screened from the casual passer-by, a path led to a sturdy little house. The oiled wood and tinted glass of the front matched the raw, primitive beauty of the spot. Stone slabs formed a path and steps up to the door. A flurry of orange and yellow nasturtiums grew over the raised basement area where the outlines of a small boat could be seen. Native flaxes and trees grew in profusion and tuis and bellbirds were chuckling and ringing their bright songs in imitation of each other. A natural clearing beside the house formed a lawn-like area.

Anna looked at Mark wonderingly. 'It looks vacant.'

'It is, at the moment.'

'Yet it's so beautiful, who could have a spot like this and bear to leave it?' she asked softly. 'Listen to the birds, it's like wonderland.'

Mark smiled at her enthusiasm. He dug his hand into his pocket and produced a key.

'It's yours?' Anna asked, as realisation dawned.

'Yes. With all the entertaining and the office at home I felt the need to have some private place of my own. There's a kitchen and ablution block at the side and the rest is lounge and bedroom in one.'

He led the way up the stone steps and unlocked the door. Inside Anna could see the gleaming wood lining the walls and the matching floor. A large divan was stretched in front of the window and a scattering of cushions in different sizes were piled upon it.

The whole of the front wall seemed to be of glass looking out towards the harbour entrance and the surrounding hills. The trees screened their position so there were no curtains to block the view. Anna sat down on the divan, her eyes on a small yacht which tacked towards the distant port. It took some moments before she became aware of Mark watching her and feeling his glance she turned and curled her feet underneath her.

'I don't think you need your hat on indoors,' he said quietly. The look in his eyes made her heart beat faster.

'Soft, silky and very sexy, Anna.' He reached out his hand and undid the knot she had carelessly fastened. His fingers brushed her throat as he undid it. The slight touch made her more aware of him. She kept her eyes downcast, determined not to respond to his magnetism. Idly he wound the silk around his fingers. She tried to sound calm.

'It would be lovely just to laze around here, you must find it hard to go back to work.'

She was proud of her words. They would remind Mark that she was his secretary and not to allow a personal relationship to develop. He nodded agreement then moved away and prepared a long drink. The ice in it reminded her to be cool. The sweet astringency of the drink made her lick her lips and she noticed Mark watching her movement and hastily looked out to sea.

He sat down beside her to point out some of the features of the hills and as he gestured she was conscious of the warmth of his body and his close proximity. Somehow she made the appropriate comments, all the time wishing that she could get up and move away. She couldn't seem to deny the feelings in her own body which had been dormant so long. Mark's black hair curled and lapped across his forehead and she almost reached out to brush it back. Instead, she tightened her hand on the glass.

He stood up to reach for a pair of binoculars and he was framed by the window against the sea. He looked like a modern day pirate with his loose limbed body and powerful, muscular chest. A moment later he adjusted the glasses and looked out to sea.

'Container ship coming in.'

He handed the glasses to her and she swept the horizon. A small dot was all that could be made out with the naked eye but with the binoculars she could see the outlines of the ship clearly.

'These are wonderful binoculars,' she commented as she tried adjusting them. The picture lost focus as she twisted it incorrectly.

'Allow me.'

Mark stood behind her and his arms held her, positioning the binoculars. Anna felt her heart beat speed, every part of her body aware of Mark's touch and his nearness. She had no idea whether the ship was still sailing the sea or if it had suddenly turned turtle; it took an effort of will to speak normally.

'That's fine.'

Mark let his arms drop and she continued to gaze at the distant sea simply because she did not dare look at him. With something like relief she picked out the ship and saw a tiny one was moving towards it.

'The pilot boat,' Mark suggested when she handed him the binoculars. 'It has gone to give the ship guidance to the port. Otherwise the vessel might end up in Taylor's Mistake or on the rocks.'

He reached down and opened the picnic hamper and within a minute spread the array on

to the low table beside the divan. Anna knew she
did not need a pilot boat to guide her in staying
away from Mark Findlay, for a woman he was
more deadly than rocks and uncharted seas were
to a ship.

He passed her a plate. 'I seem to remember you
once expressed a desire for cucumber sandwiches,' his grin was wide.

She almost choked on the memory. He had
never referred to it since the moment on the
plane.

'Thank-you.'

She hoped her voice didn't sound as breathless
to Mark as it did to her. Somehow she managed
to eat the dainty sandwich, but when Mark
offered her another she shook her head. Mark
calmly carried on eating with evident enjoyment.
Outside a tui mocked her, chuckling noisily. She
picked up the binoculars again and swept the sea.
In the short time the ship had made considerable
progress towards the port.

'It's fascinating, watching her,' Anna
murmured as Mark approached. She felt safe
behind the heavy binoculars.

'I agree,' Mark said smoothly. 'Totally fascinating. I never realised until recently. They
come and go and mean little or nothing and then
you see one and you sit up and take notice.
Whether it's the symmetry of line or simply sheer
functional capacity which impresses, I'm not
sure.'

There was a reflective note in his voice but
something else in it which made Anna look at
him.

'Silhouetted against the water the poetry of her

body is a recurring memory.' Mark met her eyes
and held them and she knew that he was not
referring to ships. She dragged her eyes away and
handed him the binoculars, not able to comment.

She had decided after Maurice that she would
never trust another man. She had gone out with a
few socially, but as soon as she felt they were
becoming serious, she had declined further
invitations. And never had she gone out with any
man from her firm. That was courting embarrassment. Yet now she was seated beside the most
dangerous man she had ever encountered, a
confirmed bachelor and a playboy and as though
that wasn't bad enough, the boss. She shook her
head. The whole situation spelt disaster.
Especially as she wanted him to kiss her.

'Why did you shake your head just now?' His
voice was low and deep and his eyes were holding
hers, his mouth only inches away. 'What were
you thinking, my cool, calm, capable Anna?'

She could not answer him. Aware of her
precarious perch she hastily slid her legs to the
ground. As though he guessed at her instinctive
desire to run, Mark took her hand. She sat very
still as he gently stroked the inside of her wrist,
the touch of his hand oddly sensuous. A ripple of
feeling seemed to course through her pulse, so
that she was far from cool, and as for calm, a tidal
wave might appear so in comparison. All she had
to do was to remove her hand from Mark's, yet
she could not do it.

Instead she felt herself turn towards him and
melt against the warmth of his body. His mouth
hovered over hers for a second and she raised her
lips. He took them slowly, deepening the touch so

that it was almost like pain, the pleasure was so rich. He released her slowly and his lips settled brief kisses on her eyes before he took her mouth again. He held her firmly, imprisoning her as desire flooded her. Breathlessly she reached her arms around him and her fingers thrust through his dark curls, as his eyes searched her face. As though satisfied, he kissed her more gently.

Anna felt a surge of love for his tenderness well up in her, it seemed to spill over to him as he cradled her. His lips nuzzled her neck and her ears and then he settled on her mouth. The kiss deepened and she felt an aching void. It was a kiss totally out of time. The sun, the sea, the hills, the trees seemed to join together, surrounding and spinning them in a blaze of light, colour, shape and sound. She felt her whole body sing and shout with triumphant joy. The relentless searching, demanding pressure of his touch slowly eased so that she lay breathless in his arms. For a long moment they simply looked at each other.

'Anna, my lovely Anna!'

Mark murmured as his hands caressed her. There was a gentleness and warmth in his voice that she had never heard before. His lips rested on hers briefly and the blue of his eyes seemed sapphire bright. The tender expression in them seemed to light his face.

As she watched she could see the shadow darken it. With a shaft of perception she knew that he was fighting his own desire for her and she could have wept, guessing that it was not his respect for her that held him back but his needs for a secretary who was capable of working efficiently. He released her and stood up in a sudden abrupt movement. She felt bereft, as though part of her had been split away. She sat up and her eyes followed Mark's athletic figure as he strode towards the door. A moment later the trees hid him from view.

She sank back on the divan, her fingers straying to her mouth as though to find her lips. She groaned softly, knowing how vulnerable she was to Mark, realising it with something like despair. If she had thrust the thought away before, now she was forced to acknowledge its simplicity and truth. She loved Mark. But Mark? He had walked away.

Mark had made his decision. The afternoon reactions had been an error of judgment and he was now standing back from the situation to see how he could rectify it.

One way would be to put in a call for Miss Penelope to fly back from her holiday urgently. Another would be to accept the half-trained girl his sister had proposed. She wondered if he would wait a day before informing her so there would be no embarrassment. Slowly Anna shook her head. Mark wouldn't care; if she wasn't up to the job she would be on the next plane home and that would be it.

There was another avenue; he could decide to wait and see if her work was affected. He wouldn't bother to send her away if it remained perfect. They were both adults. He had kissed her before at the pool at his sister's home and that had made no difference to the working relationship.

She tried to ignore the darting thought that the

kiss then had been very different from the all giving, all receiving sensation of a few moments before. Mark was a mature man, a healthy male who knew exactly what he was doing. He had read her face as knowingly as an author reads a page. She writhed, wondering if he had read her own vulnerability. Could it have been that which had made him move away from her love, with a desire to protect her? Anna knew the thought was ridiculous.

It was clear that Mark felt nothing for her and to reveal her own feelings would be pointless. She had had a very short time with him; to know him, to study his loose limbed stride; his quick lightning grin when he was happy; the serious concentration when he was reading, the puckers around his eyes where the smiles disappeared into fine lines, white against his outdoor tan; the deepness of his voice; the curling of the black hair on his forehead that her fingers had pushed back when they kissed. She pulled herself up with a jolt, knowing her thoughts were crazy.

Someday she might be able to allow herself the luxury of following along that path in her thoughts; for now the way was to be firmly barricaded. Her eyes went to the vista around her. Everything looked just the same, the blue of the gums, the red of the volcanic rocks, the green of the trees and the deep aqua of the sea. The ship they had watched earlier was now clearly visible, its progress assured.

The pilot was bringing it to the smooth waters of the inner harbour. Anna stood up. A long ago phrase came to her mind. 'Safe Harbour'.

It meant a place of haven, a secure sanctuary,

out of danger from storms. The ship seemed to know it had reached its goal.

If Mark loved her then nestling in his arms she would have felt she had reached a 'safe harbour'. Cherished and protected, able to love and give her love. But like the long ago Captain Taylor, who had sailed mistakenly into the wrong bay, she was in danger. Mark Findlay was no safe harbour for her. She had been warned; she hadn't needed navigation aids to tell her she was heading in the wrong direction, alarm signals had rung through her body. A wry smile crossed her lips at the metaphor.

She straightened and looked around. The remains of the picnic were still on the table and she packed them away, the effort of doing something numbing her thoughts. Although the basket was heavy she carted it down the steps and headed towards the car. She knew Mark would be more than willing to leave.

'I'll carry that,' Mark called. 'I'll just lock up.'

Before she had time to reach the car he had taken the basket from her. His gaze held hers and she hesitated fractionally before he spoke.

'You left your hat behind.'

He handed it to her gravely and she took it and placed it on her head. The silk scarf was folded and Mark put it down between them. It was a simple gesture but it seemed to cruelly emphasise the distance between them.

'I'll stop at the Port and see if the papers are ready,' Mark commented as they drew nearer to Lyttelton. 'If they are we can start work right away.'

She hid the pain his words caused her. She

looked at the harbour, the boats bobbing and the ships rising and falling to the breath of the water. Mark pulled up the car and the door clunked into position behind him. The facade of being uncaring almost broke as she watched him cross to the offices. It seemed to be an age before he returned. The ship she had watched earlier was now close enough for her to make out the huge containers stacked one on top of each other on deck. Soon the bright yellow container carriers would be trundling them along towards the forwarding area. The knowledge reminded her of the day she had first heard Mark's voice. Even without meeting her he had shattered her calm, she thought sadly.

Clinically she watched as he shook hands with an older man at the door of the building. His cheerful appearance told her that he had forgotten all about the emotional storm, his mind was on the papers in his hand.

'Right, we've got the permission we wanted,' he announced instantly as he opened the door. 'When we're back home you can run computer notes through to the branches giving them the details. Draft up a couple run down for Catherine so she knows how I arranged it and file a duplicate here. Don't forget the coding number for the customs.'

He was already at work despite the fact that they were driving through the white tiled tunnel. She was glad of the shadows hiding her face in the dim light. His requests would keep her busy for some considerable time. Unless she stayed on duty for several hours she wouldn't have a hope of finishing the draft, with all the cross checking it required. Clearly Mark was telling her that she was his secretary and she need expect no special treatment because he had forgotten that for a few minutes.

It was almost a relief to turn into Orakau and follow Mark to her desk. They worked together, Anna trying hard not to show the slightest difference in her manner, aware that Mark seemed exactly the same; the incident might never have happened. At seven-thirty his alarm watch pinged.

'I'm going out, Anna.' He took out his pager with a grin.

'Won't want that going off at the wrong moment. I'm not expecting any calls, but if there are any I'll check them when I return. Goodnight Anna.'

She watched him leave the office with a sinking heart. His removal of the pager told her he was not going out on business. It was some time later that she heard the car start and knew that he had left. She glared at the notes in front of her and estimated the time it would take her to complete them. So much for her own time off and the secret hope that he might have some feelings for her!

It was half past ten before she finally removed the copies from her typewriter and put them on Mark's desk for him to check. Wearily she locked up and dragged herself along to her bedroom. The moonlight in the gardens looked cool and lovely, the soft shadows of the trees etched against the ground. Reflectively she opened her door and walked out on to the grass. Some of the peace of the scene began to ease her. She wandered to the pool and sat down on the swing lounger beside it.

The realisation of her hopeless emotions attacked her again. Swiftly she stood up and ran back to her bedroom. She would swim until she was too tired to do more than crawl into bed and sheer physical exhaustion would allow her to sleep.

It took only a few minutes before she slipped into the water and began swimming. The daily practice had made it easy for her to do long distances without tiring but for once she scarcely noticed the instinctive rhythm and it was not long before she hauled herself out and sat on the end of the pool.

'Anna?'

Her name was spoken softly. She turned to see Mark, dressed only in swim shorts, standing by the entrance of the pool. His body, with powerful shoulders, gleamed. He looked like a magnificent statue brought to life by the moonlight. His muscles on his thighs and calves roped as he walked. Instinctively she wrapped the towel around her.

'Good moon for swimming,' Mark said casually as he sat beside her, his almost naked body setting her pulses racing. She forced herself to sound just as casual.

'Your party didn't work out?'

'Who said it was a party? I just decided I'd rather be home.' He looked at her and his smile was self mocking. 'You've been busy. I didn't mean you had to do that draft immediately. You could have done it in your spare time over the next week.'

'Now you tell me,' she remarked apparently flippantly. She felt pleased with her outer calm. She leaned over the pool and sprayed a cascade of diamond drops of water in his direction.

'Wretch!' He dived in and sent a wave washing over her then turned and scooped the water in giant armfuls towards her. She ran but his arm sent the water after her so she decided that being in the pool was better. She jumped in and folded her legs honeypot style so that the crash of the water splashed him.

His eyes were dark as he brushed his hand against his face, tossing the water aside. He put his palm paddle-like against the surface of the water, chuckling as he threw it accurately towards her. She responded but decided that she had made a tactical error; in the pool his size gave him a great advantage.

'Had enough?' he queried as he swam towards her.

She was panting and almost breathless as he trapped her laughingly against the side of the pool.

'To the victor, the prize,' he chuckled.

His mouth brushed hers before she even had time to realise his intention. Instinctively she pushed him away knowing she dared not let him kiss her as he had done that afternoon. He laughed, thinking it was all part of the game, but his laughter was silenced when he held her triumphantly in his arms. The touch of their wet, almost naked bodies was like an electric current flashing between them, holding them transfixed.

With a groan he scooped her against him, his sudden movement startlingly swift. His hands tightened, gripping her and his mouth took her, strong, hard and insistent.

The concrete of the pool bit into her bones as he held her, his mouth becoming gentle as she put her arms around him. Response crashed through her, leaving her weak and trembling. Mark dropped lightning kisses on her bare skin by the neckline of her swimsuit setting the pulse pounding, then he took her mouth, almost with hesitation. The sweetness of his touch throbbed through her so she was conscious only of him.

He moved a little so that he was able to study her face in the moonlight. Anna looked at him but his face was shadowed against the moonlight, all she could see was the outline of the curve of his lips.

'Darling Anna,' he whispered. 'Now you know why I wanted to come home, to you.'

His hand traced the outline of her face as though forever sealing the angles and planes into his memory. He bent forward and his lips brushed her tenderly. He released her and her balance tipped her so that she fell flat on the water. The coldness and the shock snapped her back to reality. She dared not let Mark touch her again; he was merely playing with her because she was available and he was off duty. But she hadn't kept her emotions under such a convenient lock and key arrangement. Her despairing glance fell upon the ladder out of the pool and eel-like she twisted to it climbed out and grabbed her towel, hearing Mark's chuckle, low and sensuous behind her.

Her body was still shaking but a modicum of sense told her to run to the safety of her room.

Once there she slid the door shut behind her. Her fingers fumbled with the catch and she saw that Mark had made no attempt to follow her. Rapidly she drew the curtains and was only then conscious of her wet feet marking the carpet. Hurriedly she dived for the shower. There was some release of the tension as the water cascaded over her and she pulled off her swimsuit. The faint chlorine of the pool hung about her as she scrubbed at her skin till the red marks made her realise that she could not remove the feel of Mark's touch by soap and water. Skin tingling she dried herself and slipped on her nightwear.

Yet lying in bed she could not sleep. Her thoughts, charged like activated ions, raced and crashed and spun and the more she tried to relax and not to think of Mark the more her thoughts placed him beside her.

It was late when she woke in the morning and she opened her eyes to see Sally standing beside her.

'Good morning, Anna. Mark suggested that I let you sleep. He told me to tell you only to work from eleven to twelve, the rest of the time's yours.'

'Thank you, Sally. It is nice being spoiled.'

'Well you're as bad as Mark, working all hours. Miss Penelope wouldn't do it. Mark's gone to the Christchurch office but he said he'd be back at eleven.

Hastily Anna blinked at the clock. 'Ten o'clock!' she said disbelievingly.

'You were probably overtired. Now just relax, it's a grey day and I think it's going to get worse.'

After Sally left Anna munched on the toast

happily, a secret smile in her heart at the thought that Mark had wanted to please her. Almost hesitantly a little thought came to her that he might be falling in love with her. The smile grew until it lit sparks in her eyes.

She dressed as quickly as she could and returned the tray to the kitchen. The office was open and she entered and her eyes went round the familiar room, and past it to Mark's office. Mark's pager was switched on she noticed. She felt tempted to buzz him just to hear his voice. She grinned at the thought of his reaction. She was allowing her imagination to go crazy!

Mark had left notes beside the mail and she had nearly finished it when she heard the sound of his car. She cast a quick glance at the mirror hidden in her drawer and then concentrated on the letter she was typing. Mark should find her completely composed, he was not to know that the rapid beating of her heart was covered by the rattle and click of her typewriter keys.

'Anna! Anna!' His voice was angry and demanding as he strode into the office. Her eyes flew to him and she wondered what had made him so blazingly angry. Instinctively she half-rose but backed down as he leant his arms against her desk and glared at her.

'Answer me! Did you go out with Maurice Caswell last week?'

Mark saw the truth in Anna's eyes and cold condemnation raged with his anger.

'I only met him for a short while. It wasn't a date,' Anna said, struggling to speak calmly.

'No? Just time to show how much you loved him.' His eyes glittered. 'I don't suppose you thought you'd ever see this again?'

He thumped a paper down in front of her. She opened it looking at him mystified. In a flash she realised it was a photostat copy of the important business deal Mark had worked out.

'Well, I'm waiting?'

Anna frowned. Surely he didn't believe that she had given the paper to Maurice?

'I don't understand,' she said. 'Why should I give this to Maurice?'

'Because his wife's company is an old rival; don't pretend not to know! Don't act the innocent! At least admit it!' He thrust his fingers through his hair as though he was forcing himself to control his anger.

'Are you saying I gave or sold this paper to Maurice?' Incredulously she saw from his face that her words were no surprise.

'You knew exactly how much that deal was worth to the company. I daresay you managed a fair price. As a matter of interest how much did he give you? Ten thousand? Fifteen?'

Anna felt the blood drain from her face at Mark's words.

'How can you say such things,' she asked him desperately, too shocked by his allegation to more than whisper the words.

'So, it wasn't money! What did he promise you? That he would marry you? And you believed him?'

His voice cut into her like a lash whipping her as she tried to stand while her instinct was telling her to flee. His hands gripped her arms. She shook her head.

'Mark, no! I wouldn't do it! You must believe

me.' Her eyes were agonised as she pleaded with him.

He released her abruptly and rammed his hands into his pockets as though forcing himself to keep a physical distance between them. He drew in his breath sharply. When he spoke his voice was oddly flat.

'Anna, three people knew of this deal; Catherine, you and I. Catherine had not seen that particular sheet. That narrows the field down to you or I. Maurice Caswell put it through his company. Today I found out that Clare's company was the secret purchaser. I rang Clare to congratulate her and she told me that it had been Maurice's plan. It was totally out of his field. I'm afraid I was suspicious immediately.'

He moved slowly to the desk, his anger was gone. 'It wasn't long before Clare came to see me. She had the decency to bring this paper with her. She found it in his desk. She was shocked, horrified. She had been delighted that Maurice had come up with such a brilliant idea and had agreed that perhaps after all he could stay and they would try to salvage their marriage.'

There was bitterness in his voice as he looked at Anna.

'Your idea to win Maurice's approval backfired on you, didn't it? I suppose you thought Maurice would be given a handsome bonus and you could use that as a nest egg. I've trusted you implicitly . . .'

He strode from the room as though unable to control his anger. For the first time the door of his inner office slammed behind him. The sharp bang echoed and re-echoed in Anna's mind as she sank wordlessly into the chair. The full import began to sink in.

Her eyes went to the paper Mark had produced. Someone else must have given the paper to Maurice, but who?

Anna racked her brains. Mark was right. Only to someone in their line of work would the paper have made sense. She was the only person who had access to the papers but she knew she hadn't given them to Maurice. She couldn't have picked it up unthinkingly, she was always too conscious of the paper's importance. But how did the paper get to Maurice?

Her forehead creased as she tried to remember some of the business callers. There were several but none had been left alone for a minute. Sally or John usually showed them into the reception room and then Mark would talk to them there, he seldom asked her to show guests into the office. It was impossible that one of the clients could have seen the paper, photostated it in front of Mark and calmly returned the original.

Which left a burglar, she thought sadly. Her eyes went around the room. There were many items which a burglar would prefer to a specific piece of paper. And, she asked herself, how would a burglar know the codings for the file or that Maurice would be interested in the paper? Slowly she dismissed the possibility.

Her glance went to the sliding doors which would make it easy for someone to gain entry. Several windows were under observation from the golf course, she remembered. Could one of the locals have seen someone walk into the office in the lunch hour and thought nothing of it? Perhaps even Clare Caswell?

She almost heard Clare's vituperative tone as she recalled her promise.

'It's not only golf I can beat you at, I'll get rid of you. Mark thinks you're an excellent secretary. Just wait and see. It won't be long before he's singing a different tune!'

It fitted perfectly, Anna realised. Clare was jealous of her. Clare wanted Mark, yet she needed her husband too. As a lifelong family friend she was accepted, able to visit Mark without raising eyebrows, their business a common link. And Clare had been the one to gain from the paper. She was one of the few who had walked into the office as though it was familiar territory. She had been visiting the house since childhood. It would be the work of a few moments to remove a paper from the file and photocopy it. But was it luck on her part that she had found such an important document? Anna tried to remember Clare's visits. On one of them she must have been alone in the office long enough to have studied several files.

Sadly Anna admitted defeat. She could not prove her suspicions. Maurice would never admit that his wife had been the thief, if in fact he knew a thing about the whole business. Apart from considerable financial gain, Clare had managed to win Mark's gratitude over returning the paper and his sympathy. At the same time she had succeeded in her threat in removing Anna from her post.

It would be just a matter of time before Mark asked her to vacate her desk. Tears trickled down between her fingers as she pressed her hands to her face. She tried brushing them away, but the faster she did so the more they seemed to fall.

With despair she knew it was the thought of never gaining Mark's love which caused her to ache inside. She ran to her room and lay in grief, her tears wetting the pillow. Only gradually did she gulp the sobs back and force herself to form a plan of action.

Mark would not have to tell her to go. She would leave immediately. That afternoon there would be planes flying North.

Within minutes she began packing her suitcases. The telephone by her bed was on a separate line from the office. She dialled the airport and then rang for a taxi. It would cost a fortune but she had plenty of money. Her job had been well paid and thanks to its isolation her only purchase had been the pink frock.

Anna disliked not saying goodbye to Sally and John Carter, then remembered it was their day off. Later she would write to them from the safety of her Wellington job. She stopped suddenly, aware that she could not expect Catherine Lester to employ her. She would be lucky to get a position with any other company. There would be no reference from Catherine Lester and Mark Findlay. For any employer the lack would be like a neon sign, advertising some grave fault.

She looked round the soft pastel blue tones of the suite. It was dearly familiar and she felt the sobs rise in her throat as she slipped the door behind her. With her suitcases balancing evenly in each hand she walked slowly down the tree lined drive. At the road she looked back. Orakau was lying in a shaft of sunlight as if a spotlight revealed it. Beside it the fields and paddocks formed a green and gold backdrop. Heavy clouds looked sombre as they darkened the sky. They fitted with the mood finishing the stage set.

She managed a wry smile. All she needed now was the dim throbbing and sighing of violins!

CHAPTER EIGHT

THE first spots of rain fell in fat teardrops on the taxi's windscreen. Within seconds they had formed a silver curtain the wipers had to fight to part. Visibility was cut and the taxi slowed, the driver shaking his head.

'Could see the storm coming a mile or so back. All the signs were there. It was too good to last.'

'I suppose so,' answered Anna soberly, thinking that the man's comments could apply equally to her relationship with Mark.

The trip seemed to last for hours and when the driver finally dropped her at the entrance to the airport her feelings were numb. Not surprisingly, there was a delay in all flights owing to the storm.

Bleakly staring at the dark clouds lit for flashes of time by the fork lightning, the panorama of the sky seemed to echo her own mood. Flashes of anger warred with the black misery which seemed to engulf her when she thought that Mark could believe that she had given business secrets to Maurice. Realisation began building that she would never see Mark again. Sitting in the departure lounge, she looked glumly at the ticket, telling herself that never would be quite soon enough. Contrarily she began making excuses for Mark, admitting that the evidence had been stacked against her. Circling thoughts reminded her of the moments when Mark had kissed her and the response which had flared between them.

Her hope that Mark might be falling in love with her seemed to echo with mocking laughter whenever she thought of the blazing fury of Mark's accusation. In her mind she drew the white-lipped anger, and the glitter of his glacier blue eyes as he accused her.

'Did you think you could escape so easily?'

The words were bitter and Anna gasped at the figure in front of her. He took the ticket from her suddenly nerveless fingers.

'You won't be needing that,' he snapped.

Anger at his autocratic action flashed in Anna. 'It's mine!'

'On the contrary, it's the company's,' he said icily.

Anna stood up, realising that he was right. Her ticket had been an open return one, but the Wellington office had paid for it.

'I'll concede the ticket is yours but I'll soon buy my own or reimburse you. I won't stay and be insulted by you.'

'Let's say you have a choice,' Mark drawled. 'Either you come with me back to Orakau or I shall call that policeman over there and ask him to detain you on the charge of theft as a servant. Now, if you would come with me to the baggage counter we'll collect your luggage. I presume you've already handed it in.'

Anna's eyes had opened wide in horror. 'You wouldn't!'

'I'd prefer not to,' he said quietly. The way he looked at her told her it wasn't an idle threat.

'Well?'

Stricken, she looked at him, then turned away, not wanting him to see the tears which sprang to her eyes. She stared out the window at the already parting storm clouds and the silver aeroplane on the tarmac glistened in the rain. Another few moments and she would have been safely airborne. Even the weather seemed to work in Mark Findlay's favour. A security guard walked to an outer gate and checked some item. The small action made her shiver. If she did not go back to Orakau with Mark her own freedom would be forgotten. It was as though she could see a prison wall around her. Faced with the evidence of the paper and the security of the office, no court in the land would believe her innocence. Elsewhere she could not hope to prove her case but at Orakau she might think of some way of proving that Clare Caswell had removed the paper.

Shoulders sagging, she looked at Mark. 'I'll go with you,' she said unwillingly.

'Perhaps you should hear the rest of the conditions,' he said stiffly. 'The first is to stay out of the office, the second is to have no meetings with Maurice Caswell.'

'How can I work if you ban the office?' she questioned in puzzlement.

'You won't be working, merely a temporary guest. You don't seriously imagine I could keep you on as my secretary, do you?'

'I don't understand. Why didn't you let me leave?'

'Because you could be carrying any number of private documents or information which could be of value to my competitors.'

'But that's theft!' Anna exclaimed.

'Exactly.' He turned to the staircase. 'I'll give

you three minutes to think it over. Meet me at the information desk then.'

He strode away and within seconds his tall figure was out of sight. Anna sank back on to the seat. She had thought the situation could not be worse yet the prospect ahead of her, living as a prisoner of Mark Findlay's seemed like a bizarre nightmare.

She brushed away the tears which had filled her eyes. She would not let Mark see how he had hurt her. Hastily she dabbed at her make-up, repairing the damage skilfully and then covering the telltale traces with her dark glasses. Straightening her back she walked stiff-legged to the stairs. Wordlessly, Mark glanced at her when she joined him. Her bags had already been collected, she noticed. He had known what her choice would be.

'The car's this way.'

His hands picked up the cases easily and she followed as he cut a path to the door. Magically the rain stopped as he was about to step out and within a short time they were headed down the long, flat streets leading away from the airport.

Silence hung, thick and tangible between them as the car continued back to Orakau. Mark, his jaw showing a faint, dark line of stubble, seemed like an unknown, grim stranger.

Anna gazed through the windows at the plains opening before them as they left the city behind. The storm clouds were still hovering overhead and she noticed there was no shaft of sunlight at Orakau to welcome her home.

Dry-mouthed she thought of others' conjectures.

'How do you intend to explain my presence if I'm not working?'

'Explanations should not be necessary,' he said forbiddingly.

Anna knew that Sally and John Carter would be too polite to ask, but courtesy demanded they be given some explanation.

'Would you tell Sally and John, please?'

His eyes met hers for a moment and the frozen line of his glance thawed a little.

'Very well.'

At Orakau he put her suitcase back into the blue suite. Once the door was closed Anna sank down on the bed, her whole body trembling. Only the sound of Sally and John arriving home made her spring up. Slowly she unpacked her cases.

A little later she heard another car arrive and several footsteps in the direction of Mark's office. Curiosity made her wonder what was happening, but pride made her ignore the sounds.

A tap sounded at her door and she answered it nervously.

'Anna, I've brought you in a cup of tea.' Sally's sympathetic face almost made the tears run again. 'Drink up love, just a storm. It will soon blow over. Mark used to have a very bad temper but it's the first sign I've seen of it since he was a little fellow. He'll probably apologise in the morning.'

'Thanks, Sally. You know that Mark believes I took out one of his papers and gave or sold it to Maurice Caswell.'

'He didn't mention names,' Sally said commiseratingly. 'That explains it. Young Clare will be behind it, I expect. She always did like having her own way far too much.'

'Then you don't believe I did it!'

Sally smiled. 'Don't be silly, Anna. Mark's the last person in the world you'd hurt. And even if he wasn't, you'd never do anything so dishonest.'

Anna managed a choked smile. 'Sally, I don't know how to say thank-you.'

'Drink your tea and cheer up. All we need is a way to prove Miss Clare is the one to blame.'

But that, thought Anna, was easier said than done.

Workmen were still in the corridor when Anna walked slowly down to the kitchen. One of them gave an appreciative wolf whistle as she went past, his action with the office door lock temporarily suspended. Anna felt her heart pound at the angry glare on Mark's face and it took all her courage to carry on past the door. Clearly Mark was not relying on her word to keep out of his office, he was changing the locks. She was glad Mark didn't join them for dinner, nor did he appear later. The closed door of the office told her only that he was working late.

Wearily Anna went to her room, feelings of anger and outrage fighting against her loneliness and desolation. It was a hot night and she was tempted by the thought of the pool, then remembered the happiness there the night before when Mark had kissed her. She lay awake hearing the faint whisper of the breeze in the trees and odd little night time noises. It was two o'clock before she heard the office door open and knew that Mark had at last retired for the night. Idly she wondered what business he had been conducting to such a late hour, her mind automatically checking the time zones. She grimaced, thinking of the mountain of work waiting for the next secretary to arrive.

It was the following evening before she saw Mark again. She had just finished her dinner when he entered the kitchen.

'Sally, I've decided to bring forward my trip around the branch offices. I'll be down South for a week from tomorrow and then I'll be home for a couple of nights before going North. By the time I've finished, Miss Penelope will be due home.'

Mentally Anna sighed. In many respects life would be a lot easier without Mark present but with him went her chance of proving her case. If anything went wrong while he was away it would look worse than ever. And then there was the thought that had woken her in a cold sweat that morning ... What if Clare Caswell had taken copies of several of Mark's projects? Why should she stop at one? There was another deal which they had prepared and the details had been in the new projects file as well.

Nervously she looked at him wondering if she could summon courage to suggest the danger. He flicked her with a quick glance as though to reassure himself that she was there, then turned back towards the office. Anna pushed her drink away and stood up. In the corridor Mark seemed to hesitate momentarily, then he strode towards his office.

'Mark, could I have a few words with you please?'

He turned and in the shadows his face was

grey. Anna looked up at him wondering if she had imagined the look of pain, but his expression had changed. He looked his usual, controlled self.

'Of course, Anna. Come on through.'

At the door of the office Anna hesitated and a faint curve twitched Mark's lips.

'Don't worry, I don't think you're going to filch something in front of me.'

It was an unkind insult and Anna felt tall flames rise in her cheeks. She stood in the corridor and shook her head.

'I'm not entering your office until I've been cleared, Mark. I know you believe I was the culprit so there's little point in telling you otherwise.' She eyed him steadily.

'Mark, you've always prided yourself on keeping an open mind. Your sister thinks it's one of your best business weapons. I'd like to ask you to try using it, with regard to the papers.' In the face of his gimlet gaze she quailed, but resolutely ploughed on. 'If I wanted to get more profit for Maurice I wouldn't have stopped at one paper. With it being so easy I could have photocopied several. For all you know I could have already given Maurice or some other person the details on several other files. If Clare's business could use the last file, they could equally well develop one of the new projects you'd starting working on.'

'I'm aware of that possibility,' he said shortly. 'Seeing you raised it I can ask you if that is indeed what you have done?'

'No! But I feel like it,' she said, furious with him. 'I'd like to hurt you where it counts with you—not in your heart, you haven't got one; but in your cheque-book!'

She ran down the corridor and flung herself into her room. Her heart was racing and she was shaking from the emotions which racked her. One part of her wished she'd never given Mark her warning, the other soberly tried to insist that Clare would be tempted again because of her easy victory.

It would be like the horse and the stable door, she thought sadly, there was no point in barring it after the horse had escaped. The locks would be useless if Clare already held the papers.

Her thoughts twisted round and round as she tried to imagine how Clare could have taken a pile of papers out of the house. Quite suddenly she remembered the golf trundler and bag. With that Clare could have carted out the papers right under Mark's eyes.

She had a momentary recall of John pushing away the two carts as Clare and Mark had walked together towards the house and knew that the pieces did not fit. It made her hopeful that perhaps only one paper had been involved.

She racked her brains trying to remember if the relevant paper had ever been left where Clare could have stumbled across it. There was little consolation in knowing that she was not guilty.

She pushed her fingers through her hair and noted wryly that it had grown. The wayward curl at the side fell forward and she automatically pushed it back. With pain she remembered how Mark had lifted the curl and kissed her exactly where it fell.

Lightning flashed and thunder rolled around

Orakau. Rain began beating, slashing at the windows as though in search of entry. The storm seemed to have lost little of its force. The rain was an accompaniment of the night.

In the morning she was again tempted to leave. Annoyed with herself, she sat up. Mark had threatened her with gaol and regardless of whether he was there or not she knew the threat was enough to keep her at Orakau. In many ways she could try not to loathe her prison too much. Sally and John were convinced of her innocence and their attitude had been comforting.

Bleakly she looked out. The storm clouds had gone but they had left a trail of havoc. Leaves and branches littered the grounds. John was already busy with a wheelbarrow picking up the larger pieces. Although she could do nothing about the damage to her heart, she could at least help clean up Orakau.

It was late when the three of them finally stopped working. The front lawn and side lawns were almost back to normal and John's expertise with a saw had soon neatened the split ends of the branches. The filtration of the swimming pool had been unable to cope with the sudden deluge of leaves and it had begun lapping the sides and spilling out over the paths. By the time they had mastered the system and scooped away the worst of the debris Anna was feeling decidedly worn.

'Tomorrow I'll make a start on the golf course,' John said as he put away the tools. 'I had a quick walk round and removed a couple of branches which had fallen on the greens. So long as it doesn't rain tonight I'll be able to sweep the leaves off without too much damage to the playing surface.'

'I'll help,' promised Anna. 'I've got nothing to do.'

'That's good of you, Anna. I'm sorry about the trouble.' His words were cut short as Sally called out.

'Telephone, Anna.'

'For me?'

Her heart suddenly leapt at the thought that perhaps Mark had thought over his condemnation and was ringing to apologise. She ran on happy feet and excitedly took the 'phone, smiling at Sally.

'Oh, Sally, you don't know what this means to me,' she said softly.

She could just picture Mark at the end of the line. He would be looking thoughtful, but slightly vulnerable. Unsure that she would accept his apology, she would make him squirm for at least five seconds, she decided happily. The light in his blue eyes would turn on like the sunlight on water with the glow of happiness.

Her voice was deep with emotion as she spoke, deliberately teasing him.

'Good evening. This is Anna Heathley speaking.'

'Anna, darling. What can I say? I'm so relieved to hear you are still at Orakau. Clare was sure you would have been frogmarched off the place. I thought I'd make the enquiry as I didn't know where to start looking for you. I would have rung earlier only I had to wait till the coast was clear. Clare left a short time ago to drive down to Geraldine on business. Are you all right?'

Anna kept her answer short. 'What do you

think?' she said sadly. 'I don't wish to talk to you. Goodnight, Maurice.'

'Anna, wait. I can help.'

'You've helped me quite enough already,' said Anna, suddenly remembering the fragility of her situation. 'Goodbye, Maurice.'

Shaken she replaced the receiver. Sally nodded her head sympathetically.

'You look all in. I've made you some hot chocolate, take it off to bed with you!'

'It wasn't Mark,' Anna said stricken.

'No, it wasn't Mark,' said Sally commiseratingly. 'He rang earlier while you were helping John with the last load of rubbish. Just to let me know that he's altered his schedule and gone to Geraldine tonight instead of Timaru. Apparently he's very pleased with the progress at the Timaru branch.'

'But we haven't . . .'

'A branch in Geraldine? No. Perhaps Mark's thinking of looking round there for some extra business. It's a lovely little town. I always think it would be a wonderful place for a hideaway retreat. Goodness Anna, if you don't get off to bed right away I'll have to carry you there myself. You're about as white as the wallpaper.'

Somehow Anna managed to say goodnight still clutching her drink. She went into the sweet familiarity of the blue room and let the pain claw and rip at her.

Clare had gone to Geraldine. Mark had gone to Geraldine. Mark had been pleased with the Timaru office. That was odd as the details at that branch had required a lot of extra checking and she remembered Mark's terse comments to the agent.

There was a sickening explanation to his delight. The thought of Clare in his arms made her lips tremble and a tear rolled down her cheek.

Sniffing she sought for her tissue. Clare had played her cards and she had won. From now on Anna decided that she would never trust anyone. It was a cruel twist that this time Maurice had been the innocent cause of her discovery of the truth. Again it had been the girl who had everything, as a gossip writer had glowingly described Clare years earlier on the occasion of her marriage.

'Beauty, talent, wit, charm and money!' Not to mention Mark Findlay!

There was no cheering, chirpy blackbird to wake her at dawn. The grey light crept slowly over the sky and sadly Anna watched as the sun began to flame the horizon. It was almost a relief to get up and dress in her old jeans and a jersey and begin working with John and Sally. By lunchtime the greens were tidy, but it would take time for the wounds of the storm to heal. Dumbly Anna supposed there was a lesson for her there.

Desperately she tried not to imagine Clare and Mark strolling among the gardens or swimming together or playing golf. She looked towards Sally and John conferring together on the fate of a plant and wondered what their reaction would be. Somehow Anna doubted if they would stay on at Orakau if Clare was mistress. The warm honesty of Sally would be like a reproach to Clare's guile. Mark would be generous, of course, he would probably supply them with a home of their own close at hand where John could keep a friendly eye on the new staff at the golf course. Even for Clare, Mark would not give up his friends.

They were together having tea and Anna was forcing herself to try to eat, to avoid Sally asking painful questions about her loss of appetite, when the 'phone rang. John stretched out an arm and answered the call.

'Mark! We got the greens cleared and the garden patched. Still a mess but a few days more and we should have the situation under control.'

There was a lengthy silence as Mark obviously gave him detailed instructions.

'Sure, I'll do that. Where are you ringing from?'

Anna held her breath hoping that it would be almost anywhere other than Geraldine.

'Still there? What are you up to?' A grin crossed his face. 'Even I know we haven't a branch there.'

A piece of bread lodged drily in Anna's throat and she tried to swallow. There seemed to be an enormous lump blocking the way and she made a hasty dive for the bathroom as she choked. By the time she re-entered the kitchen somewhat embarrassed, the call had been completed.

'Something went down the wrong way,' she explained. She was hoping either Sally or John would say something about Mark's extended stay in the little township but annoyingly enough Mark's name was not even mentioned again that night. Of course, nothing proved that Clare Caswell was also with Mark, but Anna knew she didn't need proof.

She was tempted to ring Maurice and ask for

his help in clearing her name. Possibly he was unaware that his wife had engineered the situation, or perhaps even he had been dismayed by her action. He had offered to help, hadn't he? Was he aware that there was more than business between Clare and Mark?

Anna tried to watch a programme on television, the flickering images as ephemeral as her thoughts.

The following afternoon Sally announced that she was tired of gardening and suggested going into town. Anna accompanied her willingly, grateful that as far as Sally and John were concerned she could do as she wished. The knowledge gave her a greater sense of freedom, but also cruelly emphasised the difference in Mark's attitude. She wondered bleakly if he would send her away at the end of the week. Surely he didn't really believe that she would remember the complicated forms and plans or that she would pass copies on to someone else? Her presence at Orakau was a constant reproach to his judgment.

Fleetingly she wondered if that was the reason why Mark had brought forward his tour. As hope spun its diamond dazzle her smile turned to a grimace. It suited him to tour while he had no secretary. It would save him time later and Miss Penelope would be due back on his return. Anna felt a little sorry for the legendary Miss Penelope. She would need all her holiday reserve to catch up on the mountain of work.

'I'm going to the hairdresser's, Anna, I'll meet you for afternoon tea at three-thirty. Will that suit you?'

'Marvellous. I want to just meander around the town.'

She was not far from the new library building and she looked enviously at several of the new books on display. Upstairs the New Zealand section interested her and she soon found several business reviews.

Flicking through the latest one she saw a reference to Mark Findlay and she read the article with a mixture of pride and anger. It gave details of the Tokyo branch office and included a picture of Mark with his Japanese agent.

Broodingly she replaced the magazine and went along to the newspaper room, intending to check the Wellington papers to see if there were any positions which would be suitable. There were two and she began noting the particulars then stopped. Until Mark let her go she would only succeed in making herself look foolish.

Discouraged she left the building and went along the small and large arcades until it was time to meet Sally. She stopped only at a bookshop for a couple of purchases.

At the coffee bar she glanced at her watch and realised that she was five minutes early. She filled in the time by writing a picture postcard to one of her friends and was just addressing it as a familiar voice hailed her.

'Anna! May I join you?'

Maurice Caswell put down his tray and sat down without waiting for her to reply. Anna remembered Mark's conditions. She was not supposed to speak to Maurice, yet she could hardly humiliate him.

'I'm still baching. Clare's had to extend her

time in Geraldine. She sounded most upset about having to go on to Dunedin. I think she may have even been missing us a little.'

He sounded so pleased at the prospect that Anna hoped he wouldn't realise the truth.

'Actually it's just as well she's away,' he continued. 'One of her new projects has suddenly gone haywire. By the time she gets back I hope to have traced the problem.' He smiled at her then spoke whimsically. 'Do you know you haven't said a word.'

Anna tried to smile. 'You always were the talker, Maurice.' Deliberately she changed the subject. 'I'm meeting Sally Carter here for afternoon tea.'

'Giving me the brushoff,' teased Maurice. 'Tell me, why did you sell those papers to Clare? I would have thought you'd be the last person to do anything dishonest. If you needed money why didn't you tell me?'

So that was the story Clare had told Maurice, Anna realised. Her coffee tasted bitter.

'I've no wish to discuss anything with you, Maurice. Just take my word I didn't sell, give or dispose of any of my employer's papers.'

Maurice nodded. 'I thought it was strange. I'll see what I can do.'

Anna was relieved. Sally approached and she waved to her to indicate her seat.

'Do you need that posted?' Maurice indicated the card.

'Yes, I'll do it later. I haven't a stamp on me at the moment.'

'Give it to me.' He pocketed it. 'I think the firm can stand the cost.'

'Good afternoon, Mr Caswell.' Sally's greeting was decidedly cool.

'Good afternoon, Mrs Carter. I'm just leaving.'

Anna hid a smile as Maurice quickly finished the rest of his drink and departed.

'Your hair looks lovely, Sally.'

'I'm pleased with it,' Sally said rather absently. The easy camaraderie between them had disappeared. Anna knew that it was due to Maurice Caswell's appearance, but she tried to tell herself that Sally must realise the meeting had been spontaneous. She set herself out to cheer and was relieved when Sally seemed more her usual self before they were ready to go home.

'I bought you a surprise, Sally,' Anna said as she handed over the latest business magazine.

'Mark gets these. I haven't seen this one about the place though,' Sally commented. She saw the photo and smiled. 'Ah! Now I understand. What a good one of our Mark. Trust him to hide the Orakau copy! Thank you, Anna. John will be most interested too. I wonder if Catherine knows it's there?'

'She usually reads it. But just in case I dropped her a card telling her to look.'

'Did you ask her to put in a word or two for you?'

Anna shook her head. She was too fond of Catherine Lester to cause friction between brother and sister. Catherine would have been given the facts. Clearly she believed Mark to be right.

'Let's go home,' she said to Sally. And only after she had spoken did she realise precisely what she had said!

CHAPTER NINE

'MARK should be home in time for dinner,' John commented to his wife at the end of the week.

Sally nodded. 'I thought I'd make him an apple pie. Remember how he used to love them.'

Sourly Anna thought that she would rather present Mark with a dish of hot chillies. All the same she found herself helping Sally with peeling the pile of apples and slicing them ready for the pie. The week had finally passed. Most of the time she had spent outdoors with John helping him clear the gardens and the golf course.

'It's hot in here, I think I'll go along and have a swim if there's nothing more I can do to help.' She turned to Sally.

'You've earned a break,' Sally smiled.

It didn't take Anna long to run to her room and change. Within a few minutes she was in the water, mentally preparing herself for the agony of seeing Mark again.

She decided she would ask him if she could leave. Surely he would allow her to go? Clare would not want her there, that was a certainty. Her lips twitched as she thought of Clare's anger at finding her still at Orakau. Possibly Mark had not even told Clare. Mark and Clare had plenty of other distractions.

Finding her thoughts on the same track again she began swimming, stroke after stroke in a determined effort to forget. When at length she

pulled herself out of the pool she looked up to see
Mark. He was still in his travelling gear, and she
guessed that he was just making his tour of
inspection of Orakau. His face was in shadow so
she could not see his expression. He looked taller,
leaner than ever.

'You've lost weight, Anna,' he commented.

With dignity she drew her big towel around
her. 'Prisoners often do, I've heard.'

Although she had rehearsed several times how
she would present her case, now he was in front
of her she was bereft of speech. Her eyes sought
his and for a second she almost stepped forward
spontaneously to him. She clenched her hands
into a fist around the towel and ran away across
the grass to the safety of her room, half expecting
him to follow her. The tension between them was
just as strong as it had been. The week's delay
seemed only to have made them more conscious
of each other.

It was harder still to appear at dinner.
Knowing the effort Sally had put into the
preparation she dressed with care. Her hair had
grown slightly longer than she had allowed it to
appear for business and the waves which were
shaped into a neat cap had begun curving into
fine curls. Her brown eyes stared back at her and
she carefully brushed on a hint of shadow.
Despite the outdoors tan she had acquired her
face looked strangely pale and she added some
blusher to hide the sign of her pallor in front of
Mark.

She made her way to the dining room warily
telling herself that she must summon courage to
ask Mark at her first opportunity. The sound of

Mark's chuckle mocked her as she opened the door. He was standing, glass in hand, smiling at Clare Caswell.

Anna felt the floor suddenly open in front of her. It was bad enough to have to attempt to eat in front of Mark knowing his opinion but to have to do so in front of Clare was worse. Hopefully she looked towards Sally and John thinking that with a guest, the staff would eat in the cosy atmosphere of the flat on their own.

'How's the golf, Anna?' asked Clare smoothly. 'Enjoying the game?'

Anna longed to give Clare's double edged words the answer they deserved but she contented herself with the observation that she had been far too busy to play.

'Never mind, Miss Penelope will come charging along soon. You haven't met her, have you?'

'Not as yet,' Anna said quietly, taking the drink Mark had poured for her and wishing she could pour it down the front of Clare's dress.

'I'm surprised you're still here,' Clare said under cover of Sally taking Mark's attention. 'Don't plan on staying much longer.'

Clare moved away to discuss an aspect of the layout of the golf course with John. Anna was almost too angry to admire Clare's sheer nerve. She wished she could go to the office and lay a tempting trail for Clare. She remembered she had said she would never enter the office and knew that even if the doors were open she would not go in. Ironically she knew that both Clare and she had the same end in view. Both wanted Anna Heathley away from Orakau!

'John and Sally told me that you've been of

great assistance,' Mark said as he came to stand beside her. His blue eyes flicked over her and rested on the curl beside her ear. Hastily Anna brushed it back.

'Leave it. I like it. That curl is a bit of a rebel. It looks as though you'll have a full scale riot of them on your hands soon.'

For a breathless moment it was as though the enmity between them had dropped away. Anna could not bring herself to answer with Mark's eyes on her mouth as though he wanted to kiss her lips. The sharp sound of a doorbell caused him to straighten and his glance suddenly became impersonal.

'Have you found my conditions too difficult, Anna? Has it been hard to stay away from Maurice Caswell?'

Anna began to formulate her answer. It was a badly phrased question, she decided. If she said 'yes' she would automatically confirm his supposition that she loved Maurice still. If she said 'No' she was not giving a truthful answer, as she had met Maurice Caswell and he had rung her as well, though neither incident had been by her choice.

'Well?' Mark was suddenly harsh, his attitude condemnatory. 'I can easily check with Sally or John. You may as well tell me the truth.'

Before she could retort, Clare interrupted them.

'Mark, darling. My ever loving husband has just arrived to pick me up. Thanks again for the ride from Dunedin.'

'I'm sure you would have done the same for me if my car had struck similar trouble.' Mark spoke smoothly. 'Evening, Maurice,' he finished as Clare's husband walked in. 'Good to see you.'

It was incredible how the polite, social conversation could sound so sincere thought Anna sickly. Disgusted, she walked out of the room to the kitchen.

'Thank goodness he's come,' said Sally grimly as she turned down an element. 'I thought I was going to have my dinner spoilt.'

'You mean Clare and Maurice are not staying for dinner?'

'No, of course not. Apparently her car broke down and as she knew Mark was coming home today she asked for a lift. Mark knows how I feel about that young woman. Her youngsters will be waiting for her at home.'

'Oh, of course.'

Outside the sound of a car engine told them that the unwelcome visitors had left.

Dinner was surprisingly pleasant. It seemed as though Mark was determined to be the most charming of hosts, entertaining Anna, John and Sally with highlights of his trip, but carefully leaving out reference to his stay at Geraldine.

Anna wondered sourly what else he was deliberately leaving out. Immediately after the meal Anna helped clear up then withdrew to her suite. She decided she would hide there until Mark immersed himself in his office. Annoyingly enough he showed no sign of wanting to work. She heard the office door clicking open but he stayed only for a few moments before returning to the lounge. The occasional rumble of laughter coming through her open ranchslider told her he was in the best of moods.

'Maybe if I asked him tonight, he'd let me go,' she muttered crossly as she picked up a book.

The memory of his earlier condemnation stopped her. She wished she had told him that he could stop playing games, that she knew he had spent two nights in Geraldine with Clare and that the affair had just carried on from there. He had blatantly driven Clare back, sure that no-one would even query the lame excuse. And apparently no-one had! The great Mark Findlay could get away with almost anything!

She wanted to go swimming, it was hot and muggy and the pool would be cool and silky, but Mark was likely to wander out and observe her. It seemed the only thing she could do was to go to bed! She didn't want to feel Mark's gaze on her again.

The night was hot and she turned restlessly, finally falling to a light slumber. Her dreams were vivid and seemed to be taking her round a coastline, searching for the right entrance to a harbour where Mark stood. Just as she was about to reach him safely, a wave of great size swept towards her. With a cry she woke up.

'Anna?'

Mark's voice was quiet in the darkness and for a moment she thought she was still dreaming. It took a moment to realise there were no mountainous seas, no ferocious clutching waves, no deceptive paths. It was a relief to wake up.

'Mark! You're real!' she said wonderingly.

A quiet chuckle answered her. 'Let me try pinching myself just to make sure.'

He sat down beside her and rubbed his chin.

'Yes, whiskers and all,' he said.

Her eyes, rapidly adjusting to the shadowy half light, saw the smile curve his mouth.

'You looked like the sleeping beauty, just now. As I remember there was one thing that reached the heart of the fair princess.'

He kissed her gently and instinctively Anna felt her magical response. With a soft sigh she wound her arms around him, threading her fingers through the dark thick hair and lifting it back from his forehead.

He kissed her lips, hovering on them as a humming bird does to a flower, so she was conscious of his maleness, the faint tang of his aftershave and the firmness of his muscular body.

'Anna, it's been so long,' he muttered as he leaned against her, imprisoning her against the pillow. His mouth deepened its pressure, responding to the eager lift of her body, taking her breath in a kiss which left her trembling and wide-eyed. Lovingly he teased the curl which fell forward on to her face, winding his fingers around it. His eyes dwelt on her hungrily before he bent to take her lips again.

'Anna, my sweet prisoner.'

The words snapped her memory. Instinctively she struggled pushing him away.

'Let me go!' Her indignant protest stilled him and she sat up, furiously pummelling him until he seized both her hands.

'Stop it, Anna. I came on your invitation, remember?'

'Invitation?' she gasped. 'What are you saying?'

'Come off it, Anna! You called out my name just as I walked past. You'd left the door wide open for me. It was a very pretty display of having a nightmare, I'll admit, only I know your acting ability of old. You're a very convincing young woman.'

Broodingly he met her eyes and shook his head. 'You're so clever you almost make me feel like apologising. In the circumstances I should have known better!'

His eyes raked her as she clutched the bedclothes around her and his lips curled scornfully. He stood up and strode to the open door. A moment later he was gone as softly as he had entered. Only the faint movement of the curtain glowing silver white in the moonlight gave a hint.

Anna put her fingers to her lips as though to stop their bittersweet tingle. Shuddering she stood up and walked to the door, remembering she had left it open for any trace of air. The click of the latch catching seemed to echo as she heard again Mark's condemnation, 'I came on your invitation, remember?'

Hours later, sleepless, she tossed and turned trying desperately to understand. Mark had kissed her as though he loved her and she had responded to him, delighting in the dream. But the dream had turned into a nightmare ... vaguely she recalled that earlier nightmare where she had been searching for a safe way of reaching Mark from the seas. Grimly she reconstructed what must have happened. Mark must have been sitting outside in the cool of the air relaxing in the quietness. She must have called out his name.

Their attraction for each other had blurred his anger and in her joy at waking to see him she had responded. It was only as he had called her his prisoner that realisation had struck. His feelings for her would have sunk to a lower ebb; before he had thought her a fraud and a thief, now he believed she had set him up to tease him physically.

At least, she decided sadly, he would be the one to suggest she caught the first plane out. She heard his car early on the morning. As she dressed she wondered dully if he would have left an envelope with instructions and her ticket with John. It was with some trepidation that she approached the kitchen, but Sally's cheerful song allayed a little of her fears.

'Good morning, Anna, did you sleep well?'

The innocent question made Anna smile wryly.

'Not exactly,' she admitted. She glanced at her empty place. No envelope was there.

'It was such a hot night, but it's going to be a beautiful day ... Mark got off to a flying start this morning. He's gone into the office in town. They'll be surprised to find him there so early. He didn't even bother with breakfast. Something had upset him,' continued Sally. 'He was worse than a dog with a bee sting on the nose.'

'Perhaps it's just the business,' put in Anna. 'He has a lot of responsibility.'

'You're as bad as John. Just making excuses for him. Mind you, we think it's a different reason altogether.' She smiled confidingly. 'John thinks he's smitten at long last.'

'Smitten?'

'You know, fallen in love. It's probably quite a shock to our man Mark. The girls were always falling all over him; it's going to be interesting to see how he likes the shoe being on the other foot.'

Anna stood rooted to the spot. 'But the person concerned might be just as keen on him,' she finally managed, thinking of Clare.

'We're not sure.'

'Oh!' She desperately sought for a way to find out if Sally was thinking of Clare as well. 'Do you think it's someone he met overseas?'

'No, Anna. It's someone close at hand, practically on his own doorstep, you might say. He's so head over heels, he can't see the hive for the bees. He's blundering around making the silliest mistake of his life.' She shook her head ruefully.

Anna tried to be flippant. 'You know what they say, the path of true love . . .'

She turned hastily to the scorching hot toast on her plate. The topic was just as hot to handle. Her toast tasted like ash in her mouth as she fleetingly remembered the gentleness of his caresses in the night. It was just as well he had called her status to mind before she had been carried away by his expertise. He was a philanderer, content to take advantage of the situation. He wasn't in love with Clare. Not if he could kiss another with so much intensity.

'. . . . so I suggested you might like to take a run. I need a few groceries as well.'

She woke up suddenly to hear what Sally was saying.

'I'm sorry, Sally, I was dreaming. Certainly I'll go for you. Just give me the list and I'll go straight after breakfast.'

'There's no great rush. I just thought you might like a spot of fresh air. Stay over there for the day. I'll get the key.'

Wonderingly Anna watched as Sally opened a

drawer and removed a key. It was instantly familiar. Mark had opened the cottage at Governor's Bay with it. Just what had Sally asked of her?

Sally began writing a list. 'There, that should do it. Pop them into the deep freeze then if John is right and Mark decides to stay there for the weekend, he'll be able to feed himself. If he doesn't there's nothing wasted.'

Anna felt her shoulders sag. The idyllic beauty of the cottage would remind her all too poignantly of Mark and her earlier visit. She wished she hadn't offered her services so eagerly. Reluctantly, a short time afterwards, she drove the car towards the town and collected a basket full of goods.

The day was hot and she felt sticky. The thought of the sea made her wish she had her bikini. Over at the beach in the privacy of Mark's domain she could sunbathe. On impulse she headed to one of the big department stores and came out smiling a few moments later, pleased with her purchase.

She headed the car towards Cashmere and climbed up the hill, stopping briefly at the Sign of the Kiwi to take in the awe inspiring view. Below her the plains stretched somnolently in the sun, wrinkling themselves to form the giant massive mountains in the distance.

She turned and the hills took her eye down to the deep blue green of the harbour below her, the tiny inlets and bays faint scarrings at the waterline. The hill led sharply down and she drove cautiously glad to arrive at the base of the hill and turn towards the beach.

The house lay tranquil surrounded by its
apparently natural clearing in the bush. Anna
parked the car and began carrying the groceries
inside. Her work completed, she filled the kettle
and switched it on. Its chirpy whistle interrupted
her reverie moments later and she made herself a
quick cup of tea and stretched out leisurely on the
divan.

The memory of Mark holding her there and
kissing her she pushed out of her mind. In front
of her the jade waters of the sea lay like a rich,
rippling silk deepening to a distant, indigo blue as
it met the sky.

Anna breathed a deep appreciative sigh. Sally
had been kind to suggest the outing. She was
safe. Mark Findlay was busy in his counting
house, he would be unlikely to think of his retreat
until five that evening and even then he would
have to drive to Orakau for the key. She looked
at it lovingly and placed it on the centre of the
table with her car keys, so she wouldn't misplace
it. So long as she held it she was totally safe. She
grinned, thinking suddenly of the three little pigs
of the nursery rhyme. No big, bad wolf would be
able to disturb her!

Feeling slightly happier she stripped and put
on her new bikini. Over it she pulled a large
towel and then stopping only to take the cottage
key she ran down to the beach. The water was icy
on her heated body until she had time to adjust to
its temperature. Soon she was basking on top of
the water, enjoying the lift of the waves which
were barely bothering to crack themselves open
against the sand and rocks of the shore. The
temperature of the water was cooler than the pool

at Orakau, she noticed, and realised that she had been so spoilt by pool swimming she had almost forgotten the joy of the open water.

A small group were swimming not far from her and she was glad of their presence. Their antics in the water made her smile and kept her mind away from a certain man. When they disappeared for their lunch she ambled along the beach looking at the differing colours of the volcanic rocks, part of long ago mountains which had formed the safe harbour around her. The magenta sweet peas she remembered were still clinging perilously along the cliffs and the bark of the bluegums flaunted the colours of the rocks.

The sea air reminded her that she was hungry and she turned away to head towards the house. Among the supplies she had bought a few extra for herself and the thought of them sped her footsteps.

Carefully hanging her damp towel over the rail to dry she reached for the key and stopped, shocked by the sight of the man who stood at the open door.

His blistering gaze made her suddenly conscious of her appearance. She stopped still.

'I didn't expect you,' she said. 'Just one moment and I'll change.'

'Don't bother on my account,' he drawled. 'You're as safe as the Bank.' His eyes glittered coldly. 'I can learn from experience.'

Anna felt the bright colour surge into her cheeks at his words. She hesitated, longing to tell him that he could think what he liked and storm off, but her brain quickly told her that Mark would put it down to histrionics. It would serve no useful purpose. Her clothes and the car keys were inside and to get them she had to go past the mocking figure.

Anna flinched at the expression in his eyes. Coldly blue they seemed to freeze her and strip her at the same time. The colour flared in her cheeks under his annihilating glance.

'Please let me pass, Mark,' she said with an attempt at dignity. 'I'll just get my clothes.'

'Go ahead,' he commented. He moved down the steps leaving the way clear. Hastily Anna pulled on her clothes, uncaring as to the state of her hair or make-up. She reached for the keys she had left on the table, then realised they were not there. She frowned wondering if she had taken them to the beach with the cottage key. Puzzled she looked under the table then remembered she had sat on the divan. She looked underneath then sat on top while she tried to remember.

'Looking for these?' Mark held the keys and she knew instantly he had taken them deliberately.

'Could I have them please, Mark, then I'll get out of your way.'

'Not until I want you to leave,' Mark said softly, his voice ringing danger signals to her ears. 'What were you doing here in the first place? Searching for more secrets?'

'If I said that I'd been stocking up your larder would you believe me?'

'That's probably only an excuse you thought up to give to Sally. Why not tell the truth? What was Maurice Caswell doing here?'

'Maurice? Here?' Surprised Anna could only stare at him. 'I've no idea in the world. Where is he now?'

'He's left,' Mark said shortly. 'He went over to Orakau to see you this morning and Sally told him you were here. Then I rang and she let me know that he was on his way to see you.'

He spun suddenly so that he was gripping her arm.

'Why, Anna, why did you do it?'

'Do what?' For a moment she was shocked by his anger. 'What are you implying?'

'I'm saying that you supplied Maurice Caswell with further information.'

'That's ridiculous! How could I? I haven't touched your office since the new locks were installed.'

'Only because you couldn't get past them,' he said with a ferocity which made her shiver. 'You had already taken what you needed before the locks were installed. Just one other paper worth even more than the first.'

'Why didn't you search my bags?' Anna asked bitterly. 'Then you'd know I was innocent.'

'I had my own way of checking. I altered the codings to protect the files and I also took some precautions for the other deal on the projected list. However, as you didn't know you weren't able to tell him.'

His eyes glittered. 'I guess that's why Caswell came running to find you this morning. His calculations would have gone haywire. When Clare finds out you'll be lucky if he's still in one piece.'

Anna followed his figure as he moved towards the window, his back to her.

'Just how much did he give you?'

'Nothing, for the simple reason I had nothing

to do with removing the papers. I wouldn't do it.'

Her voice sounded flat and uninspired. She felt she couldn't fight any more. She had warned Mark against the very possibility of the plan having been removed at the same time, yet he still blamed her.

'Stop pleading innocence. I'm tired of it. I'd have thought that this morning, at any rate, you'd have admitted the truth.'

'I have told you the truth. What evidence have you?'

'Clare found the first paper herself on Maurice's desk. And for the second piece of information I can thank Sally.'

'Sally?'

'Yes. When I asked her she told me that whilst I was away Caswell had rung you and also that you had met him in town. She was sure it was quite innocent but then Sally doesn't understand the stakes you were playing for, does she? She told me you had given him what looked like a letter. Shall I tell you what Sally overheard.' He paused and looked at her, enunciating each word clearly. '. . . the firm can stand the cost.'

Anna put her head in her hands. She knew she was beaten. Clare Caswell had completely outmanouevred her and Sally had played right into Clare's hands.

'It was a postcard of the Town Hall and the cost involved was a stamp,' Anna explained.

Mark's lips curled in disgust. He dropped the car keys on to the table and the clink seemed noisy.

'If you drive to the airport you'll be able to

pick up a ticket and your luggage at the enquiry desk. Leave the car keys there. I don't wish to see you again.'

Anna looked at him, dry lipped. The dark curls lay on his forehead but there was none of the little-boy-lost look about him. His face was shut against her, the expression in his eyes as they met hers flared flame-like, but he turned and opened the door.

Trembling, Anna picked up the keys. Tears filled her eyes but she would not dash them away while Mark could see the movement and guess the cause. Somehow she managed to walk down the steps knowing that she was walking out of Mark Findlay's life. Yet it was the last thing she wanted to do.

It took her a long time to gather strength enough to drive the car and head towards the airport. She parked the car and locked it and walked determinedly to the building. The dark glasses she had worn for the sun earlier, now hid her tear-washed, red-rimmed eyes from the others waiting in the concourse. The girl at the enquiry desk told her the luggage had already been put aboard and urged her to hurry as the last boarding call for her flight had been given a minute earlier. Somewhat bemused she joined the tail end of the passengers walking to the waiting plane.

An hour later the taxi was taking her through Wellington's familiar streets. Instinctively she found her eyes going to the office building near the waterfront, the capital city's home for Mark Findlay International.

Past the line of the harbour the cab crawled in the traffic and Anna could not restrain the tears that ran down under her glasses as she looked at the sea. Azure blue it reminded her of the harbour at Governor's Bay. She remembered Mark telling her that it had been named after Governor George Grey, who had waited there to welcome the Canterbury pilgrims in 1850. After their long, perilous journey it must have seemed a safe haven. For her it had proved to be the opposite. She wouldn't venture into the deep oceans of love again.

It was strange waking in the morning and knowing there was no urgency to get to the office. She lay in bed trying to work out her plans, but always she found her thoughts returning to Mark Findlay. Determined to thrust the thought away she began to organise her future. Her bank balance was healthy; being Mark's secretary had been financially rewarding and he had continued her salary automatically whilst she was staying at Orakau. She would return that money, she decided. Mark felt she had been paid enough!

Her eyes swept the situations vacant columns of the morning paper and she ringed two positions.

Thinking of the prospective positions reminded her of the thrill she had felt at becoming Catherine Lester's secretary. From the beginning they had worked well together and she had been delighted with the added opportunities Catherine had given her. Her lips pulled a rueful curve as she recalled Catherine's promise to train her as an agent. Although there was an age difference she had really enjoyed Catherine's friendship and she was disappointed that her former boss had not supported her and known Mark's allegations to be incorrect.

Sighing, she crackled the newspaper to shake her thoughts away from the circle and turned the page. The business pages she had found fascinating since her work with Mark Findlay International. Many of the companies conjured up pictures of people she had met. Finished, she determinedly pushed the paper aside and seeing her suitcases decided to unpack. It had been too much of an effort the night before but now it had to be done.

Putting away the meticulously folded garments made her think of Sally and John. She wondered what they would have thought on being told that she would not be returning to Orakau. Sadly, Anna pulled out the last dress and saw the letter sitting in its folds. Puzzled she turned it over and saw her name in Sally's characteristically neat hand on the envelope. It hadn't been sealed and she pulled out the page wondering.

'Dear Anna,

John and I are very upset with the news. I feel badly about it as I was trying to explain your comments to Maurice Caswell but Mark seemed determined to misinterpret my words. I was trying to hint that I was sure there was nothing to your relationship with Maurice and I'm very much afraid I only made things a great deal worse. I feel sick as Mark has asked me to pack your bags. I've never known him so furious. Remember me telling you that the storm would pass; just to stay and enjoy

yourself with us and to ride it out? It seems I
landed you in the middle of a tornado which
will blow you away. With Mark's black anger
you might be better in Wellington for a few
days, I'm sure it won't take him any longer to
work out what he has done and why he reacted
so badly. John suggests you practise your golf
shots while you've got the chance. We're both
looking forward to welcoming you back to take
your rightful place at Orakau.

Sally and John.'

'Oh, help, I'm turning into a waterworks,'
muttered Anna as she put down the letter. She
felt tremendously warmed by the loving affection
that showed in it. She sniffed and blew her nose
then re-read the note. The last sentence made her
sigh. Evidently Sally and John expected her back
as Mark's secretary but even if he found out the
truth she would not go back to Orakau. Miss
Penelope was expected back by the time Mark's
tour was over.

She pocketed the letter, then realised that she
was not surprisingly very hungry; she had
scarcely eaten for twenty-four hours. With her
appetite restored a little by the letter she
prepared a quick meal. It took her only a few
minutes to eat then she began to tidy the
apartment. She would throw out every reminder
she had of Mark Findlay.

The buzz of the door bell made her stop her
flurry of activity. She hesitated, thinking of her
dishevelled appearance, then automatically flat-
tening the curl which danced round her ear, she
answered the door.

'Catherine!'

'Anna, my dear, I don't know what to say. Really, my brother has done some oddball things in his time, but never any mistake quite so disastrous. Why didn't you tell me what had happened?'

'You mean you didn't know?' said Anna, her brows creasing. Suddenly realising that she was keeping Catherine on the doorstep, she ushered her inside.

'Well, of course I didn't know! I rang Mark this morning only to be told he was still over at the Bay. That's surprising enough at nine o'clock in the morning but then I asked Sally why you hadn't answered the 'phone and she told me you'd been sent back to Wellington! You can imagine how I felt! My own secretary flown back and no-one told me! Then Sally began on this long, detailed explanation that Mark thought you'd sold or given papers to Maurice Caswell. What a load of nonsense!'

'Oh, Catherine!' Anna found her tears traitorously welling to the surface.

'There, Anna, you couldn't have thought I'd believe it?'

'There was no word,' put in Anna simply. 'And your brother is the boss. The evidence looks bad.'

'Piffle! I don't care how much the evidence is stacked against you, Clare Caswell has obviously been up to her usual tricks.'

'Then you . . .' Anna was silent.

'Blame Clare? Yes, of course. I know that young woman of old. "The leopard doesn't change her spots", as the saying goes. I've never known her to do anything affecting the business before, but she did pull a couple of nasty stunts whenever a girl came close to Mark. She always wanted him herself, but he wasn't interested and I think it's annoyed her ever since.'

Catherine eyed her secretary with a great deal of satisfaction. Anna found the colour rising in her cheeks at the inspection.

'So you must have presented the worst danger yet! I suppose in a way it's a back-handed compliment. Clare must have been furious when Mark kept you at Orakau after the first incident.' Catherine Lester chuckled. 'I can just see her claws!'

'Well, I felt them,' said Anna with a wry trace of humour.

'Yes, I'm sorry, Anna, really you've been through a dreadful time. You should have rung me or told me on that card. Instead of that "Wish you were here".'

'I didn't like to say anything as I didn't want to cause trouble between you and Mark. I did wish I could see you so that I could explain. It hurt that you believed such a thing. Then it backfired. The postcard I sent you was the mystery letter Sally saw me give Maurice to post. The words were about the firm standing the cost of the stamp.'

'So that's what it was. Why didn't you tell Mark?'

'I tried,' she managed.

'So at the moment you could wish Mark Findlay at the bottom of the sea!'

'That's the safest place I could think of!' Anna muttered wrathfully.

Catherine laughed delightedly. 'Oh good, then all's not lost. You're over him already. I can see that. So there's no reason why you can't start work,' Catherine said with sudden decision.

Anna looked at her former boss in surprise. 'You want me to come back, now?'

'This minute won't be too soon. I know it's asking a lot but I would appreciate it, Anna.'

'But what about Mark? He won't like it,' Anna said hesitatingly.

'He'll just have to put up with it. He made me responsible in the Wellington office. Don't forget I'm the second biggest shareholder.'

'No, Catherine, I don't think I should. I can't tell you how much it means to have you trust me but . . .'

'Nonsense! The way to clear your name is to come back. You do want to do that, don't you?'

'Yes, of course.'

'Right, change out of your Mrs Mop outfit and come on. I warn you, you'll be working late tonight.' Catherine Lester smiled. 'I'll give you five minutes.'

There were times, reflected Anna an hour later when she found herself back in the luxurious Wellington office, that Mark and Catherine were very alike. It seemed they both had the ability to make people do exactly what they wanted.

That morning she had lain in bed worrying about a job and a work reference and now she was up to her elbows in work. It seemed as if Catherine had been saving up the countless memos and files. She was glad to be busy, the work kept her thoughts occupied and she was forced to admit that Catherine was right. At least in the office of Mark Findlay she might be able to prove her record.

In time the truth had to appear. Her only hesitation came when she answered the telephone. Each time she wondered if it was Mark who was calling and what his reaction would be to her presence. She could only be grateful that he would have left the Bay that day for the Auckland office. His tour would keep him fully occupied. Not that she was interested, in him, she told herself. Clare Caswell could keep him!

A week later Anna was looking down at the harbour scene when the telex chattered. Obediently she picked up the strangely coded memo and walked into Catherine Lester's office.

Catherine read it and clearly understood the news.

'Anna, I'm flying down to Orakau. Can you book me on the next plane South?'

'Is something wrong?' White fear hammered at Anna as she visualised Mark lying stricken on a road, or lost at sea, or . . .'

'No, it's just a spot of cooking.'

'Cooking?'

Sheer astonishment widened Anna's eyes.

'That's right.' Catherine smiled, clearly pleased with herself. 'Cancel my appointments for the next two days will you? Reschedule them for the beginning of next week if you can. If it's urgent I'll be available at Orakau. You've worked like a little beaver getting all those notes up to date. Once you've rescheduled the appointments take the time off. I don't want you near the office, clear? Go and rest, or,' her eyes twinkled, 'practice your golf. I'll be back on Friday evening probably.'

'Would you like me back here on Friday?' asked Anna.

'No, Monday will be fine. I'll give you a ring over the weekend if I don't see you before. Use the pool at home if you feel like it. You've probably missed the pool at Orakau.'

Anna nodded, her throat suddenly constricted. The pool was the least of the items she had missed. The boss of Orakau had troubled her far more.

Anna was still curious about the 'cooking' by the end of the week. Apart from a mystery telegram which declared the geese were in the pot, no word had come from her boss. Anna had taken advantage of the time to spring-clean her apartment. As well, she had kept herself occupied shopping for the oncoming autumn. She was pleased with an elegant, soft, woollen dress in a subtle, pale green and she had also bought a tweed suit which would be perfect for the office.

She began thinking of Mark again and resolutely she turned her mind away. She wasn't going to dream of 'might have beens' any more. If Mark Findlay had known how desperately she loved him he would have known she could never have sold the business secrets. If he had loved her he would never have formed the liaison with Clare Caswell.

'Stop it,' she lectured herself. 'Stop thinking of Mark! It's over. Grow up!'

She thumped a cushion into position then smiled ruefully. It was just as well no-one was there to hear her talking to herself! Glumly she stared at the view over a patch of a neighbour's garden. The very sight of the colourful gladioli made her think of the large bunches of them windswept and broken at Orakau by the storm.

She shook her head, realising that every thought kept on bringing her back to the same point. Mark looking at her, the dark curls falling forward on his forehead and his blue eyes, dancing and sparkling with humour, then his expression changing as he bent to kiss her . . .

The sharp ring of her doorbell interrupted her thoughts. She moved forward wondering which one of her friends had come to visit.

'Mark!' Shock forced the word out in a gasp as she opened the door.

'Good afternoon, Anna. May I come in?' His face was tanned and his blue eyes seemed deeper than ever. He stood as though uncertain, on the door step.

'I'd throw my hat in first, only I don't wear one!'

With the automatic gesture she knew so well, he thrust his hand through his curls sweeping them back. Anna was surprised to find herself opening the door wider.

'Come in,' she said quietly, ignoring the warning of her body. She didn't know how much she could take if Mark was to begin accusing her again.

'I've come to apologise, Anna. I was wrong. I'm sorry.'

His words were so unexpected she could only stare at him.

'I'm sorry, Anna. I think I was crazy. When I found out the truth I realised what a fool I'd been. I'm not sure what to say.'

His blue eyes held hers for a moment and she

felt her heart leap. She forced herself to look away. Silence twanged between them.

'Catherine showed me the postcard you'd sent. I remembered your explanation and later Maurice verified it. That's when the penny dropped. I remembered Clare knew all the files as well as you. Clare also had access. When I charged her with it, she admitted it.'

'But you believed Maurice and Clare and not me.' Anna's eyes held shadows.

'I don't think I wanted to believe you,' Mark answered her slowly. He turned to the window. 'You see, I'd fallen in love.'

The blow had struck. Anna winced in pain. She could understand Mark's feelings. He had fallen in love with Clare, only to find her a cheat and a thief. It would have been preferable to believe his temporary secretary was the culprit.

'It's too late, isn't it? I've ruined everything with my blind stupidity.'

Compassion for the loneliness and the pain and hurt she could read in him tore at her.

'I'm sorry, Mark,' she said gently.

He bowed his head to hide the suffering in his eyes. A moment later he spoke again.

'It's ironic, isn't it? This morning after we'd signed the contract to buy Clare's company someone asked me how I felt. I told him there was little joy in the acquisition, only work. At least I have that.'

Anna looked at him wondering if she had heard correctly.

'You bought Clare's company?'

'Yes, I had considered buying a couple of Clare's offices in Geraldine and Dunedin, and

Catherine worked out such a great deal Clare was screaming for mercy! On top of my booby trap of the second paper, Clare decided she'd had enough. In the circumstances I was able to make their departure a condition of the contract. Maurice, Clare and the children leave for Europe at the end of the week.'

Surprised, she looked at him. 'They're leaving? Forever?'

'Yes.' His answer was brief. Anna realised that buying the business had sent Clare away, despite his love for her.

His discovery had sharpened his perception of others' feelings, she noted. He straightened. His face wore its usual businesslike expression.

'Now, on the subject of compensation. I have decided that you have every right to it. I have caused you considerable "pain and suffering" as the court puts it.' He pulled out an envelope from an inside pocket. 'There's a cheque enclosed.'

He put the envelope on the table as Anna looked at him in horror. It seemed the final insult. He was paying her off. Angrily she picked it up.

'You can keep your money,' she flared, ripping it into shreds. She marched to the door. 'I don't want to hear or see you again! Just go!'

His face went pale under the tan, but he strode past her wordlessly and walked down the steps. Anna slammed the door behind him then leaned against it, her body sagging as though she had just run herself to exhaustion. After a few minutes she bent to pick up the pieces of the envelope and cheque. She would put it in with the rubbish and that would be the end of the matter. It was a great pity she couldn't dump Mark Findlay on top of the pile!

Glancing down she saw the amount and her eyes widened. She assembled it jigsaw-wise and smoothed it out. There was no mistake. Mark Findlay was making sure she had no cause to go to the law. She doubted if even a court would have given her such an amount. Mark was not worried about his name, she knew that instinctively. It was Clare he was protecting, Clare he was concerned about. Clare whom a court would find guilty. Clearly he had hoped the cheque would mean she would be able to leave the country without prosecution.

Anna gathered up the pieces and swept them into the rubbish. She had no intention of bringing an action. All she had hoped to do was clear her name and now that had been done. So why was she crying?

It didn't help to know the answer. Mark Findlay loved Clare. Anna scrubbed at her eyes. She grabbed a light jacket and thrust it on. Stopping only long enough to pick up her keys she set off down the road. Her feet were beginning to tire when a bus pulled in beside her to let a passenger alight. Hurriedly feeling for change she found the fare and took the first, free seat. The bus carried her over the familiar roads towards the city. It stopped right outside the Ferry terminal and the sight of the sea brought a longing to her heart.

A seagull called in the sky above her and she turned to watch it as it hovered until joined by its mate. Together the two flew until they were hidden by the buildings. A bright-eyed pigeon alighted clumsily on a post beside her and bent its head at her with a look of enquiry. Satisfied, it turned and preened itself, the rainbow of magenta on its neck iridescent against the grey. The colours reminded her again of the little Bay she had loved with Mark. She frowned to catch her thoughts and stood up.

Looming skywards was the office building, the insignia of Mark Findlay on the side. She took out her keys and checked she had the office one on her ring. Resolutely she walked towards it. Right now she would collect her bits and pieces and set her desk in order for the next occupant. She could not work for Mark Findlay and she knew Catherine would understand.

The caretaker was washing the ground floor foyer and he nodded a greeting to her as she fitted her key to the lift. It whisked her to the double wooden doors and she fitted her key and flicked on the lights. In her office she began emptying her drawers and relining them. There was little of her own, a small bottle of her favourite perfume which she put on automatically before pocketing it, some make-up and her own large dictionary. Finished, she sat at the desk and pulled out the pile of work she had prepared ready for Catherine's attention. To make sure they were not forgotten she put them on top of her desk.

She began drafting her resignation. It was a difficult letter to write:

'Dear Catherine,
I can't go on working here. I'm sorry. I think

you're a fasntastic person and I shall always be
grateful for your support and your trust. But I
can't stay. I've been stupid and fallen in love
with Mark . . .'

She read it, pulled a face and yanked the paper
from the typewriter and began again:

'Dear Catherine,
I wish to tender my resignation. Thank you for
your trust in me . . .'

She stopped as the computer chattered and
clicked. Surprised she left her desk and looked at
the message wondering if Catherine was sending
it from Orakau just on the off-chance of someone
being at the office.

'That's for me, I believe.' She spun round at
the sound of Mark's voice. He came from
Catherine's office.

'What are you doing here?' she squeaked in
surprise.

His eyebrows raised. 'I could ask the same of
you.'

He went towards her desk and glanced at the
letters.

'It's a letter of resignation,' Anna explained.

'Yes.' His tone was non-committal. 'I thought
it might be. I don't suppose I can ask you to stay
on here. I'll get Miss Penelope to send you a
reference as soon as she arrives.' He gestured to
the pile on her desk.

'Do those need attention?'

'Yes. Catherine went off to Orakau in such a
hurry.'

'Now you know why.' There was a trace of a

smile. 'I'll check these in a few minutes.' He picked them up and took them into Catherine's room.

Shaken, Anna looked at her desk. Her heart was beating and sheer reflex action helped her finish the formal letter. As she unplugged the machine she looked round for the first draft.

Aghast, she realised that Mark must have picked it up with the pile. She could only hope that he had not begun reading it. Somehow she had to get it back.

Haunted, she opened Catherine's door. Mark was seated on the desk, his long legs swinging. Even as she watched he picked up the first page. Mortified she recognised it.

'Oh no, please, Mark.'

Wildly she clutched at the paper but he held it out of reach. She knew then that he was already reading it. The colour of humiliation seeped through her cheeks. Mark glanced at her, his face tender.

'You love me?'

His tone was incredulous, uncertain, as though unable to believe the words in front of him. Anna wanted to turn away but he forced her to look at him, his hands gentle as they turned her face. Again almost hesitantly, he repeated the question.

'You love me?'

Anna was trapped. She wanted to say 'No,' but honesty would not allow the easy way out.

'Yes.'

'My darling Anna.'

He let the paper go and drew her towards him,

holding her as though she was a delicate piece of porcelain. His lips went to touch hers but instinctively Anna pulled away, her body rigid with shame. Fat teardrops spilt from her eyes.

'Sweetheart, what's wrong?' Mark was surprised. 'What's the matter?'

Numbly she could only look at him.

'Anna, it's all right. Whatever is wrong we'll fix it between us. So long as we love each other we'll be happy.'

'But you don't love me?' Anna forced out the words in pain. 'What about Clare?'

'What about her? It's you I love; not Clare.'

'Me?' Hope soared like a giant white bird in her heart, only to crash as she remembered Clare's relationship with Mark.

'Darling, you're looking at me as if I'd suddenly turned into a fat toad!'

'Don't you call me darling! I might have been a fool to fall in love with you, but I'd be a worse one if I believed you. I suppose you call Clare "darling" too!'

'You're jealous!' crowed Mark. 'My own wonderful Anna! I assure you there's nothing to be jealous about. Clare was an old friend of the family, as children we were close and she was my first girlfriend. Later I lost interest. I saw more of her lately as the Dunedin agent had tipped me off that I might make a good purchase of her business there and in Geraldine. I wanted to keep it strictly business, but . . .' he hesitated and Anna saw him search for the words. 'Clare had other ideas. Once I would have had few scruples, but I kept seeing your eyes and remembering your face. I couldn't pretend, Anna. You'd spun a magic spell around me and no other woman meant anything.'

He stopped and saw the blaze of joy on Anna's face as she realised the truth.

'Oh, Mark!' she spoke almost breathlessly.

Anna saw his eyes bright blue before she closed hers as Mark tenderly drew her into his arms and his mouth took hers. Passion, fired by the intensity of their emotions, deepened the kiss, making it all giving, all demanding, all shattering!

Mark released her and his hand swept the curl which danced coquettishly by her ear. His mouth dropped a kiss on it before he took her lips again, hovering over them sweetly, then moving to leave kisses like tiny sparks on her eyelids.

'My sweet, wonderful Anna,' he said softly. 'I'm yours just as much as you are mine.'

Anna knew his words were true. Love had told her, as it had told Mark. Glowing with happiness, she fitted into the curve of his arm. She felt cherished; loving as well as loved.

Behind them, the big window showed the port and two ships which had just arrived. Smiling, Anna knew they too had found 'Safe Harbour'.

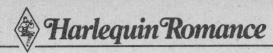 **Harlequin Romance**

Coming Next Month

2755 CINDERELLA WIFE Katherine Arthur
The idea of pretending to be the adoring wife of a powerful fashion mogul is bizarre. The possibility of having to give him up in a year is heartwrenching.

2756 GIRL OF MYSTERY Mons Daveson
An Australian millionaire is mystified by a secretive waif who dashes in front of his Jaguar. She won't tell him her address; so he feels compelled to take her home.

2757 AEGEAN ENCHANTMENT Emily Francis
A physiotherapist loves Greece! But her patient's older—and hopelessly overbearing—brother insists she will never understand their ways and can't belong. Which only makes her more determined than ever to fit in.

2758 HUNGER Rowan Kirby
When a Canadian writer and his troubled daughter invade an English bookshop owner's solitude, can she balance her hunger for love with her fear of being hurt again?

2759 PAGAN GOLD Margaret Rome
Valley D'Oro's mining magnate accuses a visiting Englishwoman of squandering her family's fortune to trap a man of substance. Yet he defends his family tradition of purchasing brides from impoverished aristocrats!

2760 SKY HIGH Nicola West
An amateur hot-air balloonist refuses to be grounded by an unfair job interview. She knows exactly where she wants to be: suspended somewhere between heaven and earth—in this man's arms.

Available in April wherever paperback books are sold, or through Harlequin Reader Service.

In the U.S.
P.O. Box 1397
Buffalo, N.Y.
14240-1397

In Canada
P.O. Box 2800, Postal Station A
5170 Yonge Street
Willowdale, Ontario M2N 6J3

You're invited to accept 4 books and a surprise gift Free!

Acceptance Card

Mail to: **Harlequin Reader Service®**

In the U.S.
901 Fuhrmann Blvd.
P.O. Box 1394
Buffalo, N.Y. 14240-1394

In Canada
P.O. Box 2800, Postal Station A
5170 Yonge Street
Willowdale, Ontario M2N 6J3

YES! Please send me 4 free Harlequin Romance® novels and my free surprise gift. Then send me 6 brand new novels every month as they come off the presses. Bill me at the low price of $1.65 each ($1.75 in Canada)—an 11% saving off the retail price. There are no shipping, handling or other hidden costs. There is no minimum number of books I must purchase. I can always return a shipment and cancel at any time. Even if I never buy another book from Harlequin, the 4 free novels and the surprise gift are mine to keep forever.

116 BPR-BPGE

_____

Name   (PLEASE PRINT)

_____

Address   Apt. No.

_____

City   State/Prov.   Zip/Postal Code

This offer is limited to one order per household and not valid to present subscribers. Price is subject to change.

ACR-SUB-1R

WORLDWIDE LIBRARY IS YOUR TICKET TO ROMANCE, ADVENTURE AND EXCITEMENT

Experience it all in these big, bold Bestsellers— Yours exclusively from WORLDWIDE LIBRARY WHILE QUANTITIES LAST

To receive these Bestsellers, complete the order form, detach and send together with your check or money order (include 75¢ postage and handling), payable to WORLDWIDE LIBRARY, to:

In the U.S.
WORLDWIDE LIBRARY
901 Fuhrmann Blvd.
Buffalo, N.Y. 14269

In Canada
WORLDWIDE LIBRARY
P.O. Box 2800, 5170 Yonge Street
Postal Station A, Willowdale, Ontario
M2N 6J3

Quant.	Title	Price
_____	**WILD CONCERTO**, Anne Mather	$2.95
_____	**A VIOLATION**, Charlotte Lamb	$3.50
_____	**SECRETS**, Sheila Holland	$3.50
_____	**SWEET MEMORIES**, LaVyrle Spencer	$3.50
_____	**FLORA**, Anne Weale	$3.50
_____	**SUMMER'S AWAKENING**, Anne Weale	$3.50
_____	**FINGER PRINTS**, Barbara Delinsky	$3.50
_____	**DREAMWEAVER**, Felicia Gallant/Rebecca Flanders	$3.50
_____	**EYE OF THE STORM**, Maura Seger	$3.50
_____	**HIDDEN IN THE FLAME**, Anne Mather	$3.50
_____	**ECHO OF THUNDER**, Maura Seger	$3.95
_____	**DREAM OF DARKNESS**, Jocelyn Haley	$3.95

	YOUR ORDER TOTAL	$_____
	New York and Arizona residents add appropriate sales tax	$_____
	Postage and Handling	$___.75
	I enclose	$_____

NAME _____

ADDRESS _____ APT.# _____

CITY _____

STATE/PROV. _____ ZIP/POSTAL CODE _____

WW-1-3